Hi, Parents!
Your child's love of reading starts here, with HarperAlley's I Can Read Comics!
HARPER alley

**I Can Read *Comics*** introduces children to the world of graphic novel storytelling and encourages visual literacy in emerging readers. Comics inspire reader engagement unlike any other format. They ask readers to infer and answer questions, like:

1. What do I read first? Image or text?
2. Why is this word balloon shaped this way, and that word balloon shaped that way?
3. Why is a character making that facial expression? Are they happy, angry, excited, sad?

From the comics your child reads with you to the first comic they read on their own, there are **I Can Read *Comics*** for every stage of reading:

**LEVEL 1**
Simple stories for shared reading.

**LEVEL 2**
Engaging stories for children reading on their own.

**LEVEL 3**
Complex stories for independent readers.

The magic of graphic novel storytelling lies between the gutters.
Unlock the magic with…

## I Can Read *Comics*!

Visit **ICanRead.com** for information on enriching your child's reading experience.

# I Can Read *Comics* Cartooning Basics

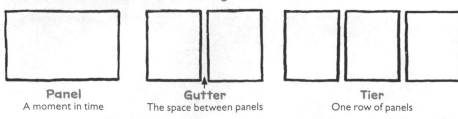

**Panel**
A moment in time

**Gutter**
The space between panels

**Tier**
One row of panels

**Word Balloons** When someone talks, thinks, whispers, or screams, their words go in here:

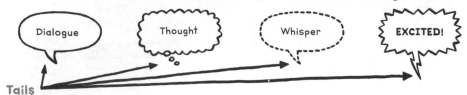

Dialogue   Thought   Whisper   EXCITED!

**Tails**
Point to whoever is talking / thinking / whispering / screaming / etc.

## A quick how-to-read comics guide:

In a **panel**, read the text on the **left** first.

Then, read the text on the right.

### Remember to...

Read the text along with the image, paying close attention to the character's acting, the action, and/or the scene. Every little detail matters!

### No dialogue? No problem!

If there is no dialogue within a panel, take the time to read the image. Visual cues are just as important as text, so don't forget about them!

On a page, **start here**, in the **top left** corner!

After that, read the panel immediately to the **right**.

When you're done up there, come down here and read **this** panel **next**!

ME NEXT! ME NEXT!

You're almost there...

YOU MADE IT! You just read a comic page!

YAY!

*For my husband, Will, for always being there to help —S.W.*

HarperAlley is an imprint of HarperCollins Publishers.
I Can Read® and I Can Read Book® are trademarks of HarperCollins Publishers.

Tiny Tales: A Feast for Friends
Copyright © 2022 by Steph Waldo

Library of Congress Control Number: 2021945761
ISBN 978-0-06-306786-8 (trade bdg.) — ISBN 978-0-06-306785-1 (pbk.)

Book design by Joe Merkel
21 22 23 24 25   LSCC   10 9 8 7 6 5 4 3 2 1   ❖   First Edition

# LEVEL 3

# I Can Read!
## Comics

# Tiny Tales

## A FEAST FOR FRIENDS

by Steph Waldo

HARPER alley

An Imprint of HarperCollinsPublishers

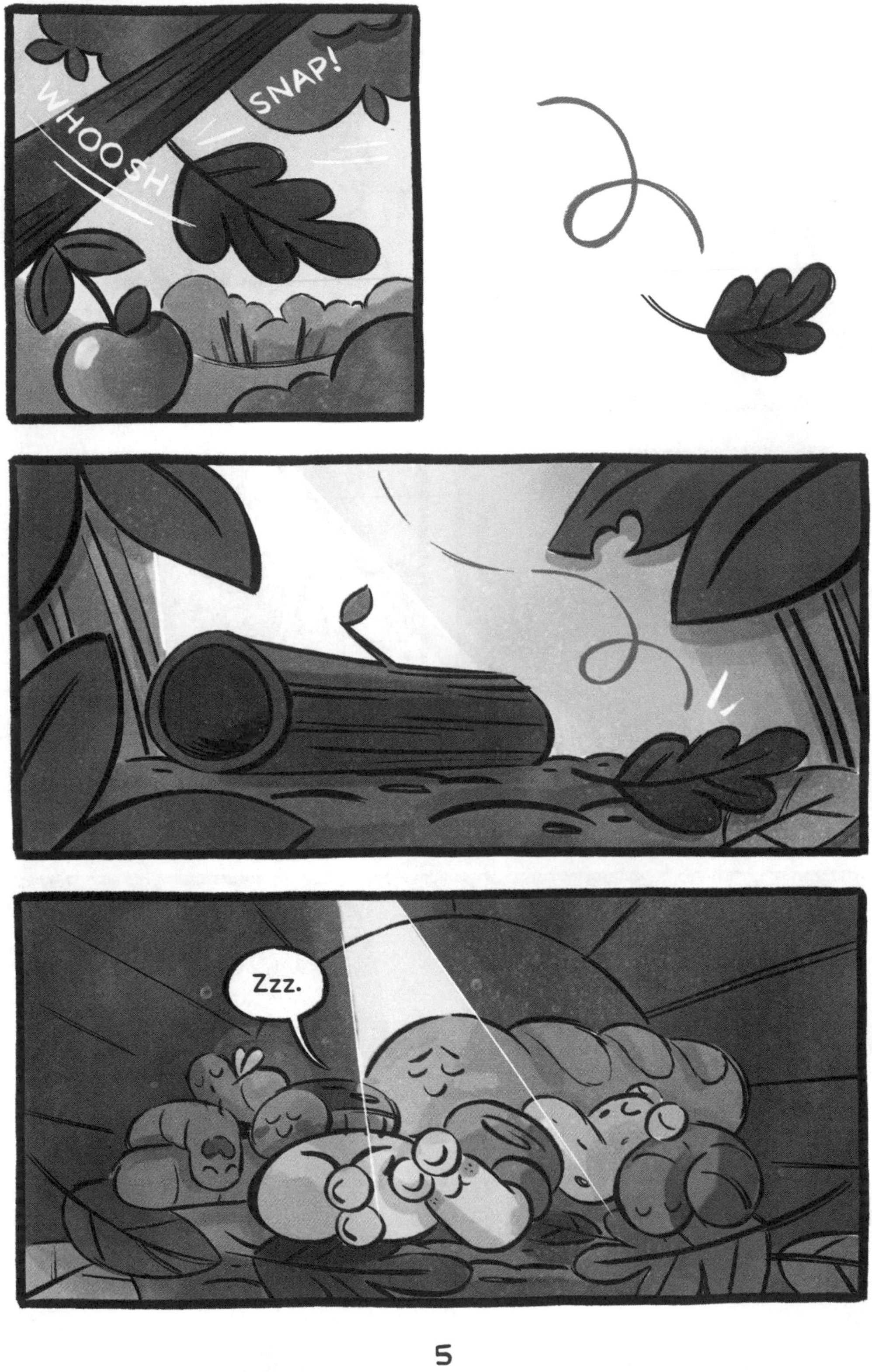
WHOOSH
SNAP!
Zzz.

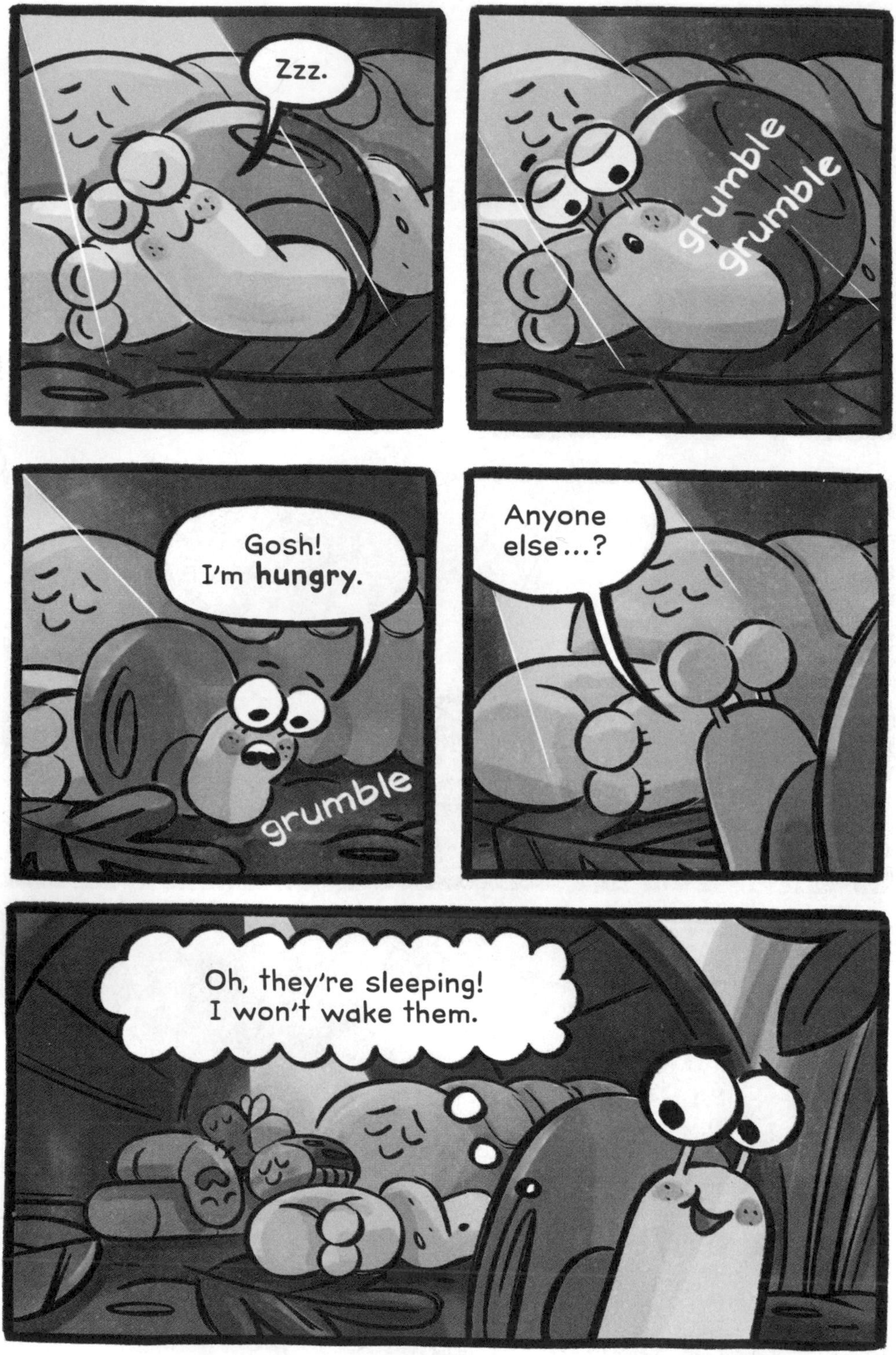
Zzz.
grumble
grumble
Gosh!
I'm **hungry**.
grumble
Anyone else...?
Oh, they're sleeping!
I won't wake them.

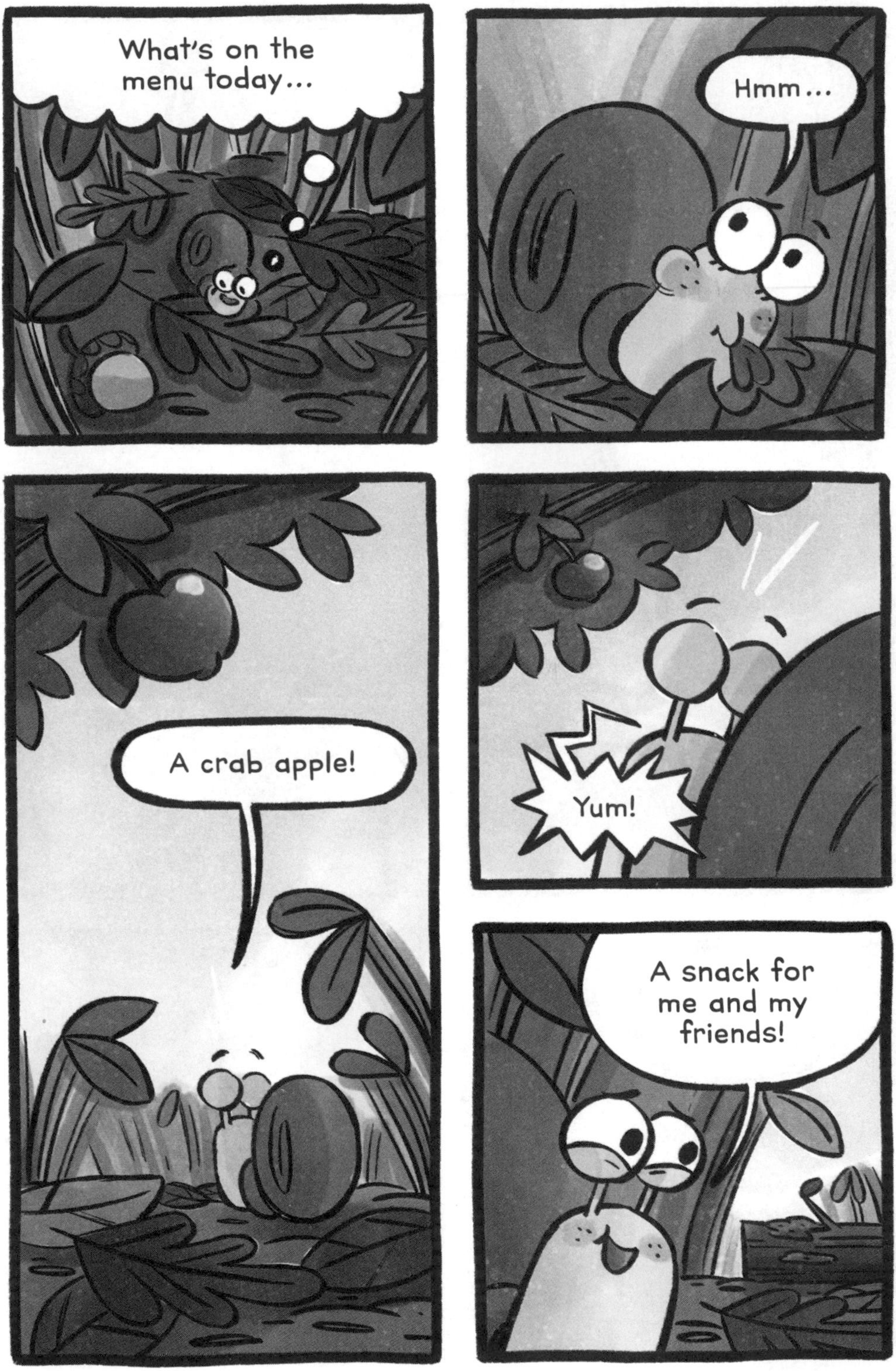
What's on the menu today...
Hmm...
A crab apple!
Yum!
A snack for me and my friends!

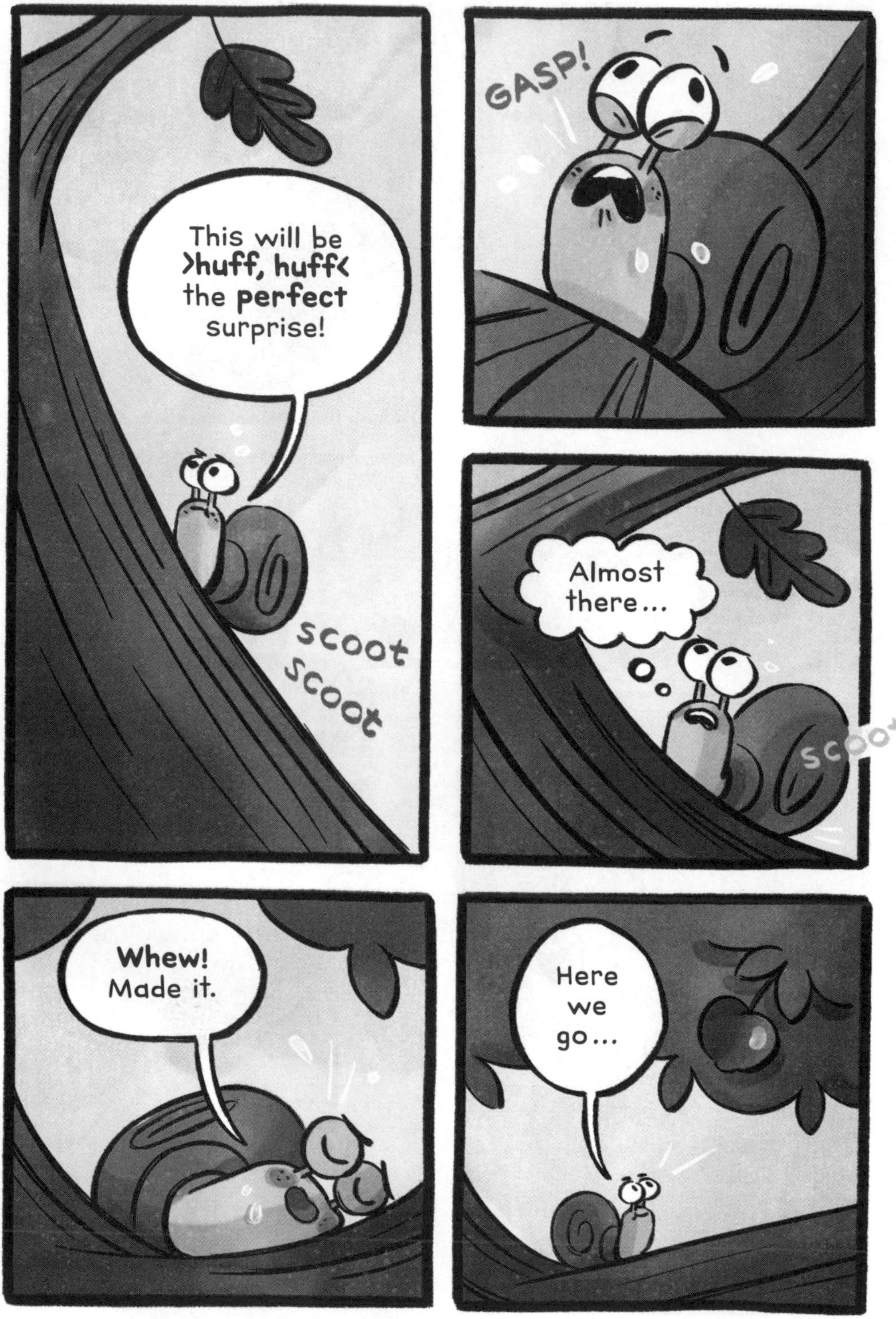

This will be >huff, huff< the perfect surprise!
scoot
scoot
GASP!
Almost there...
scoot
Whew! Made it.
Here we go...

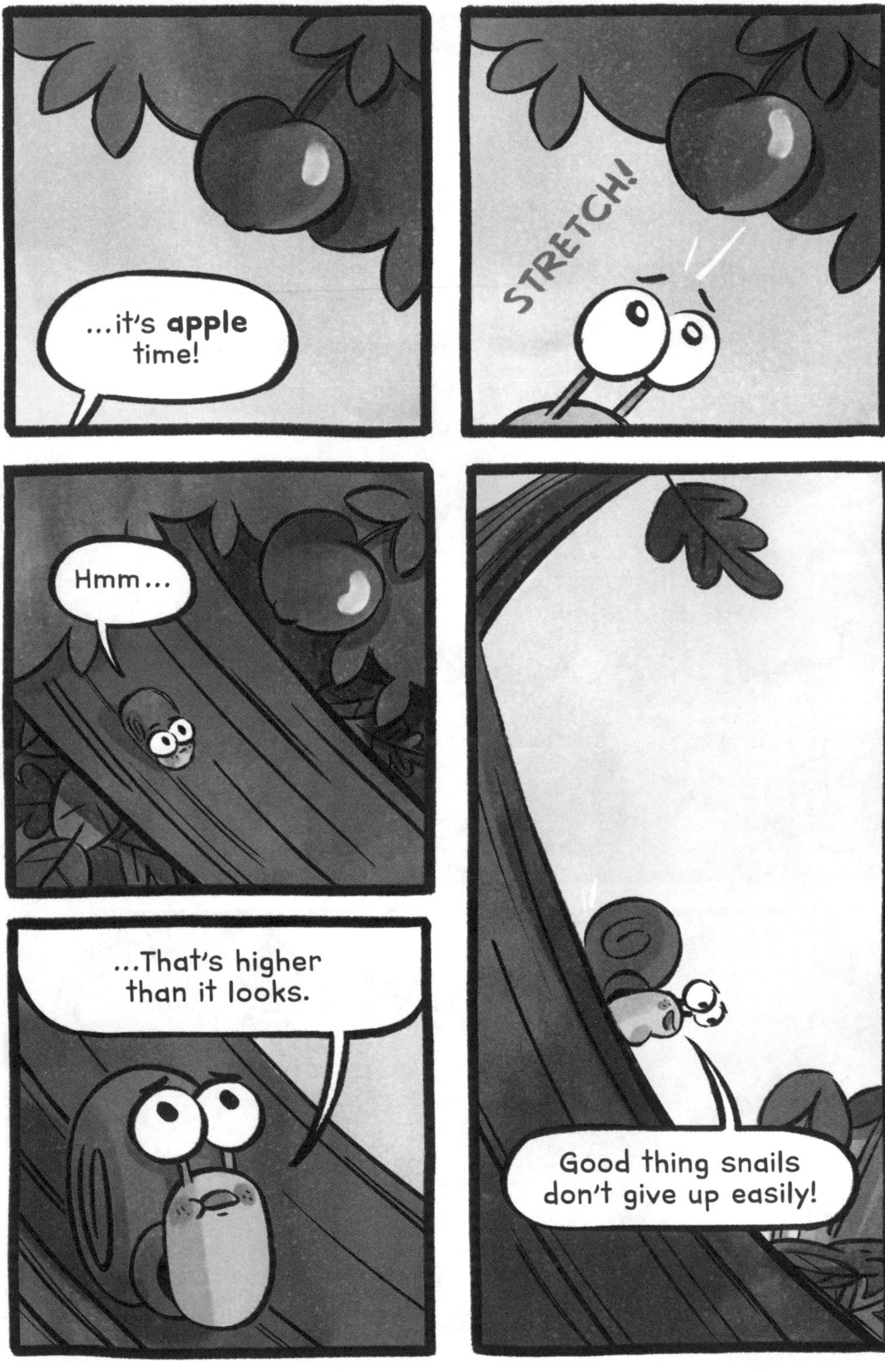
...it's **apple** time!
STRETCH!
Hmm...
...That's higher than it looks.
Good thing snails don't give up easily!

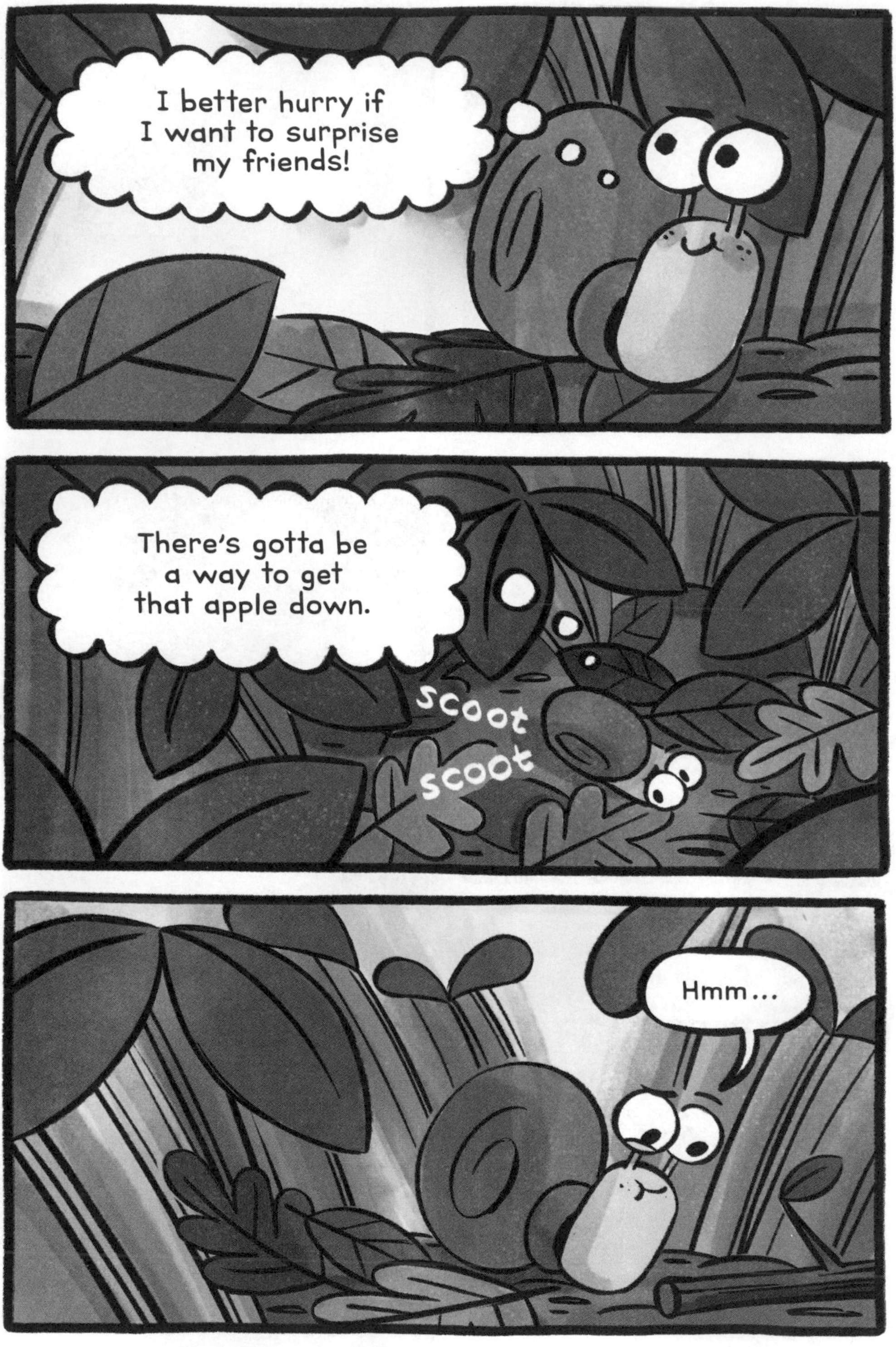
I better hurry if I want to surprise my friends!
There's gotta be a way to get that apple down.
scoot
scoot
Hmm...

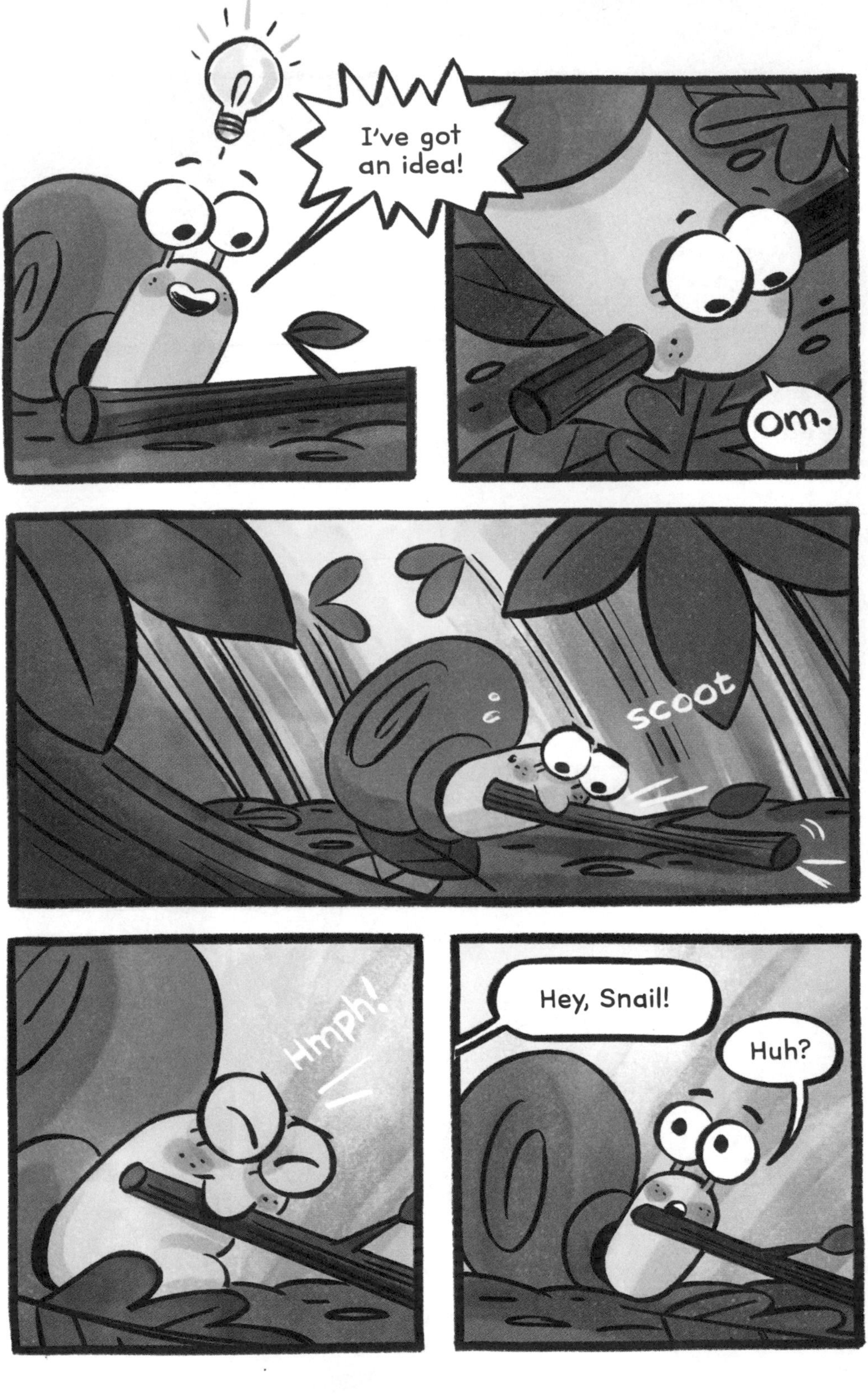
I've got an idea!
Om.
scoot
Hmph!
Hey, Snail!
Huh?

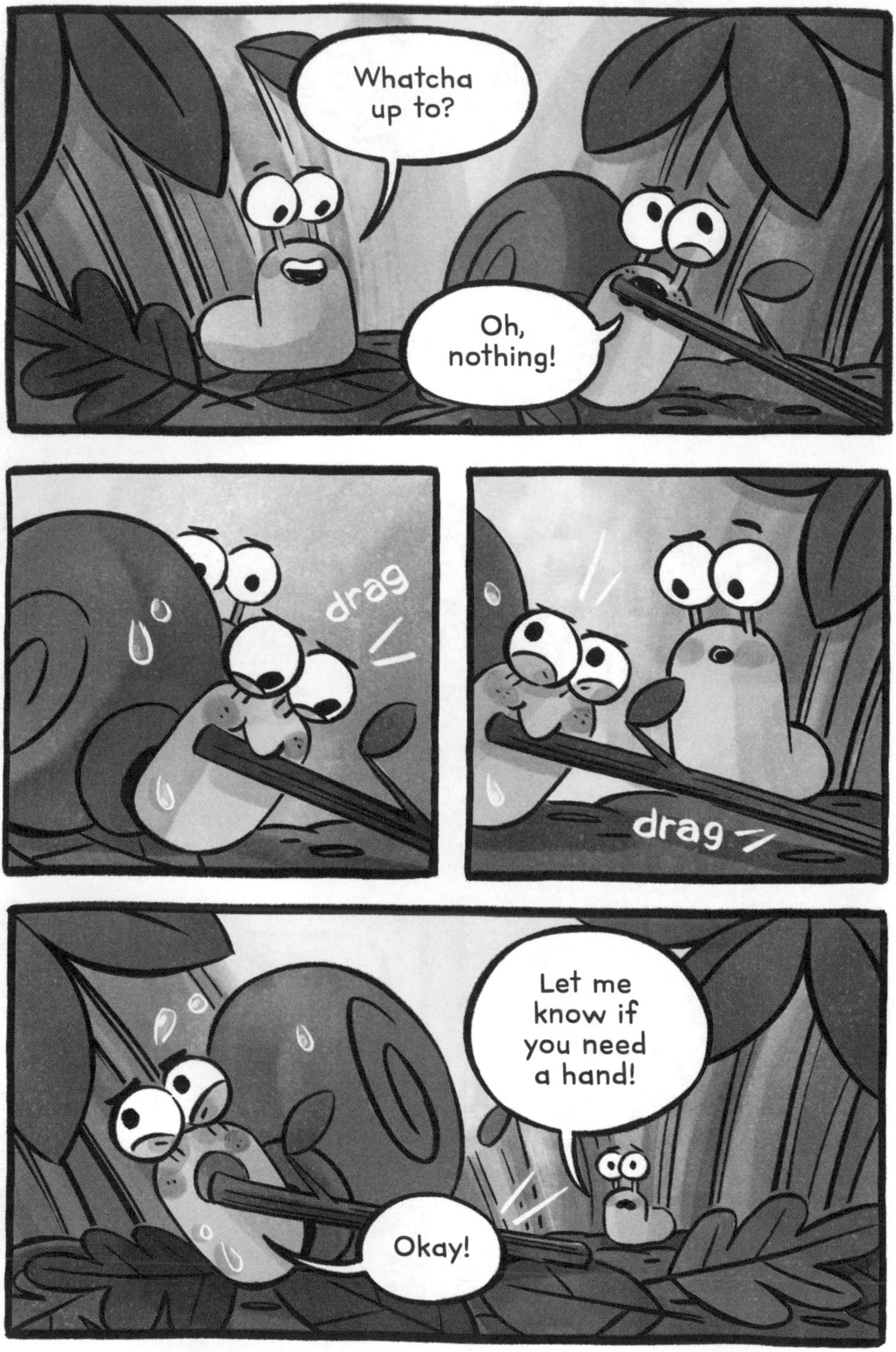
Whatcha up to?
Oh, nothing!
drag
drag
Let me know if you need a hand!
Okay!

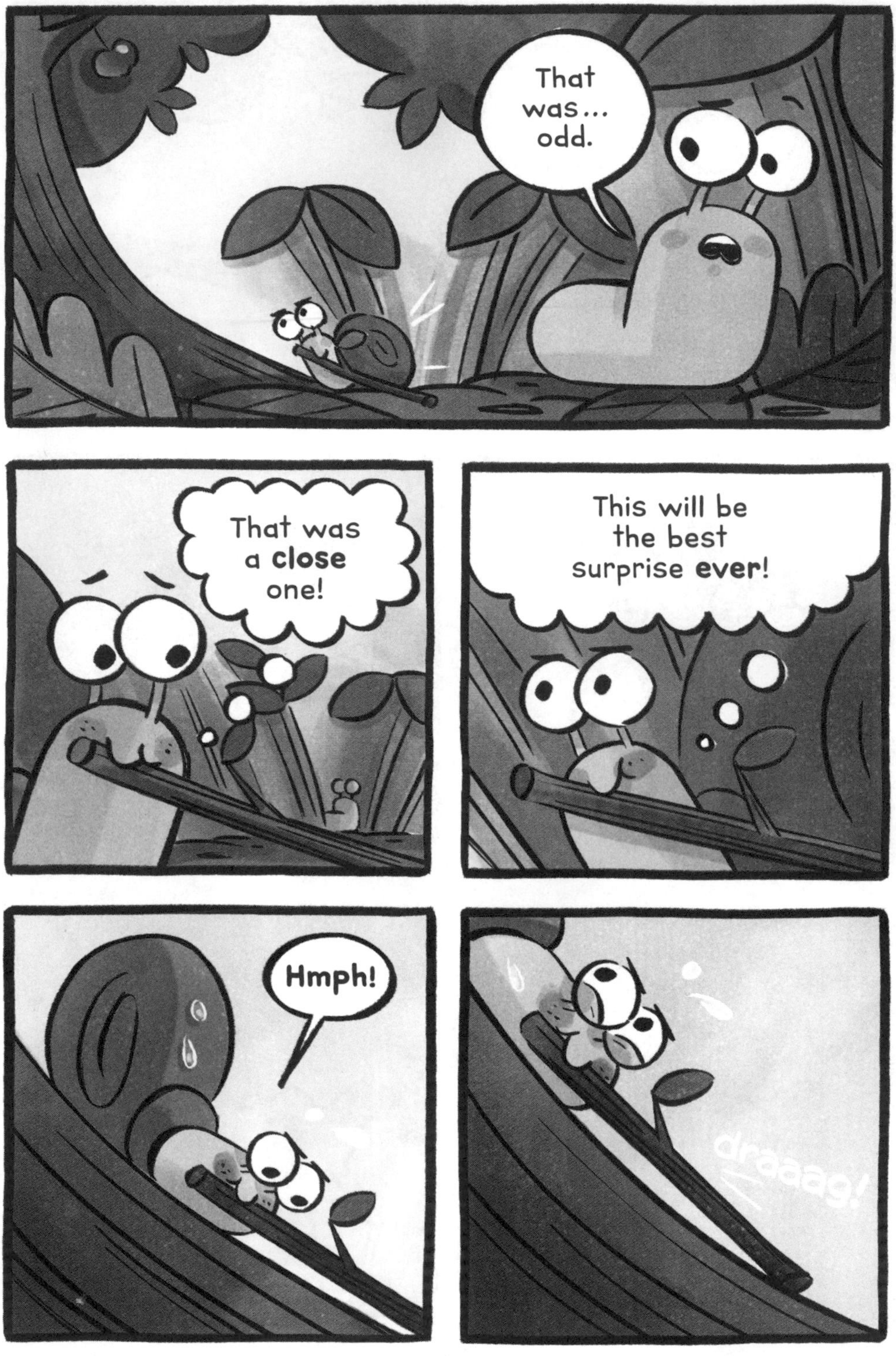
That was... odd.
That was a close one!
This will be the best surprise ever!
Hmph!
draaag!

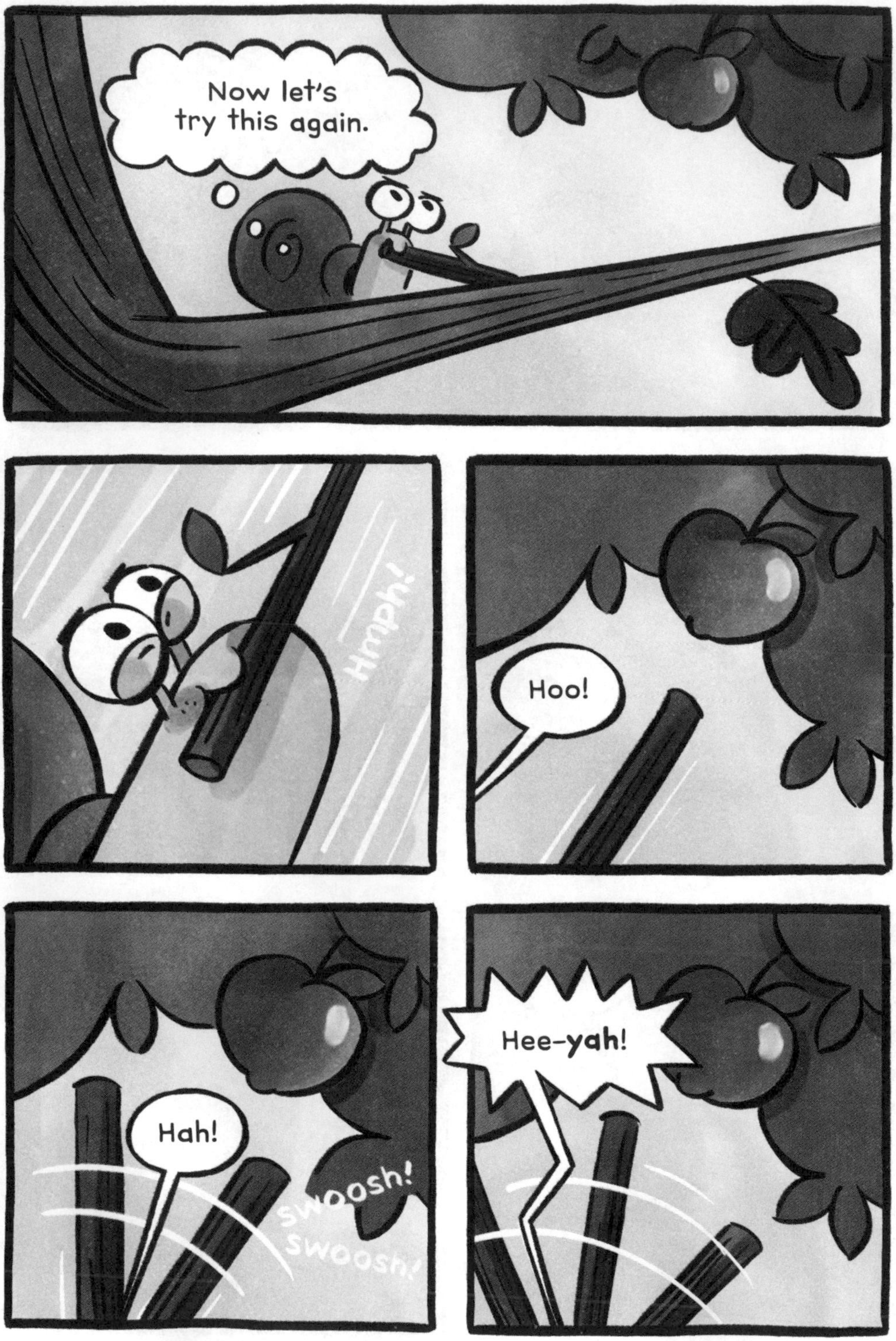
Now let's try this again.
Hmph!
Hoo!
Hah!
SWOOSH!
SWOOSH!
Hee-yah!

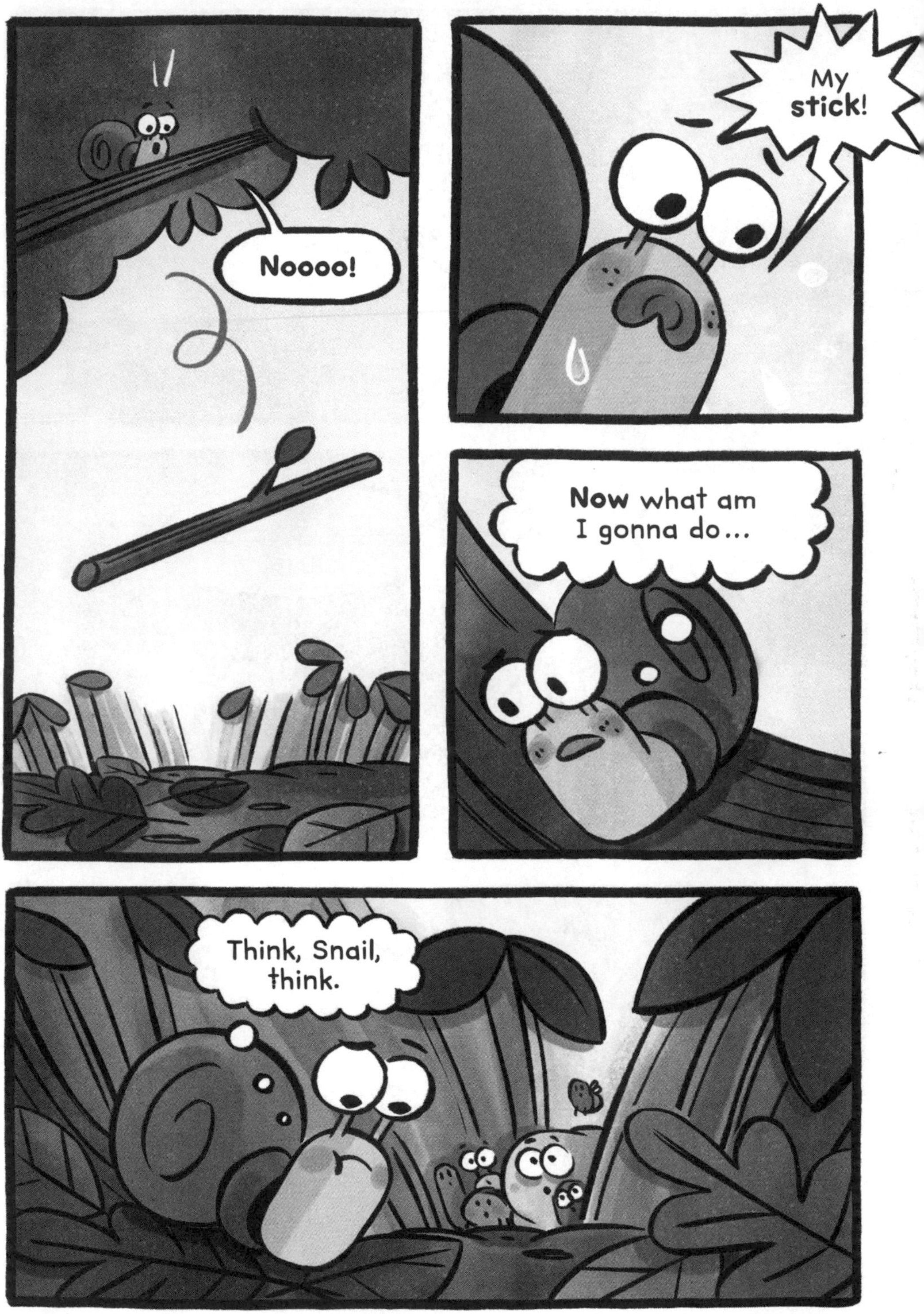
Noooo!
My stick!
Now what am I gonna do...
Think, Snail, think.

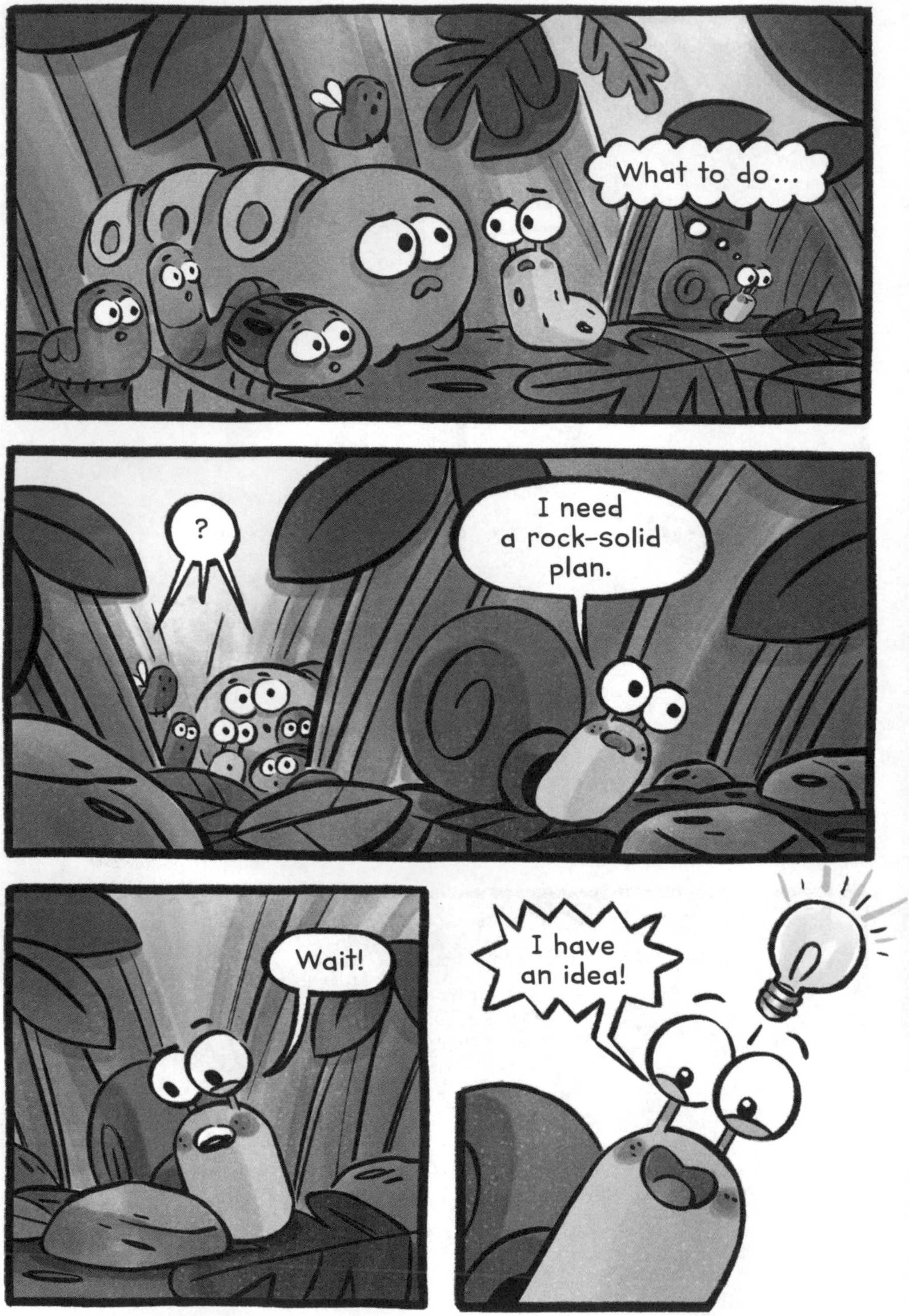
What to do...
?
I need a rock-solid plan.
Wait!
I have an idea!

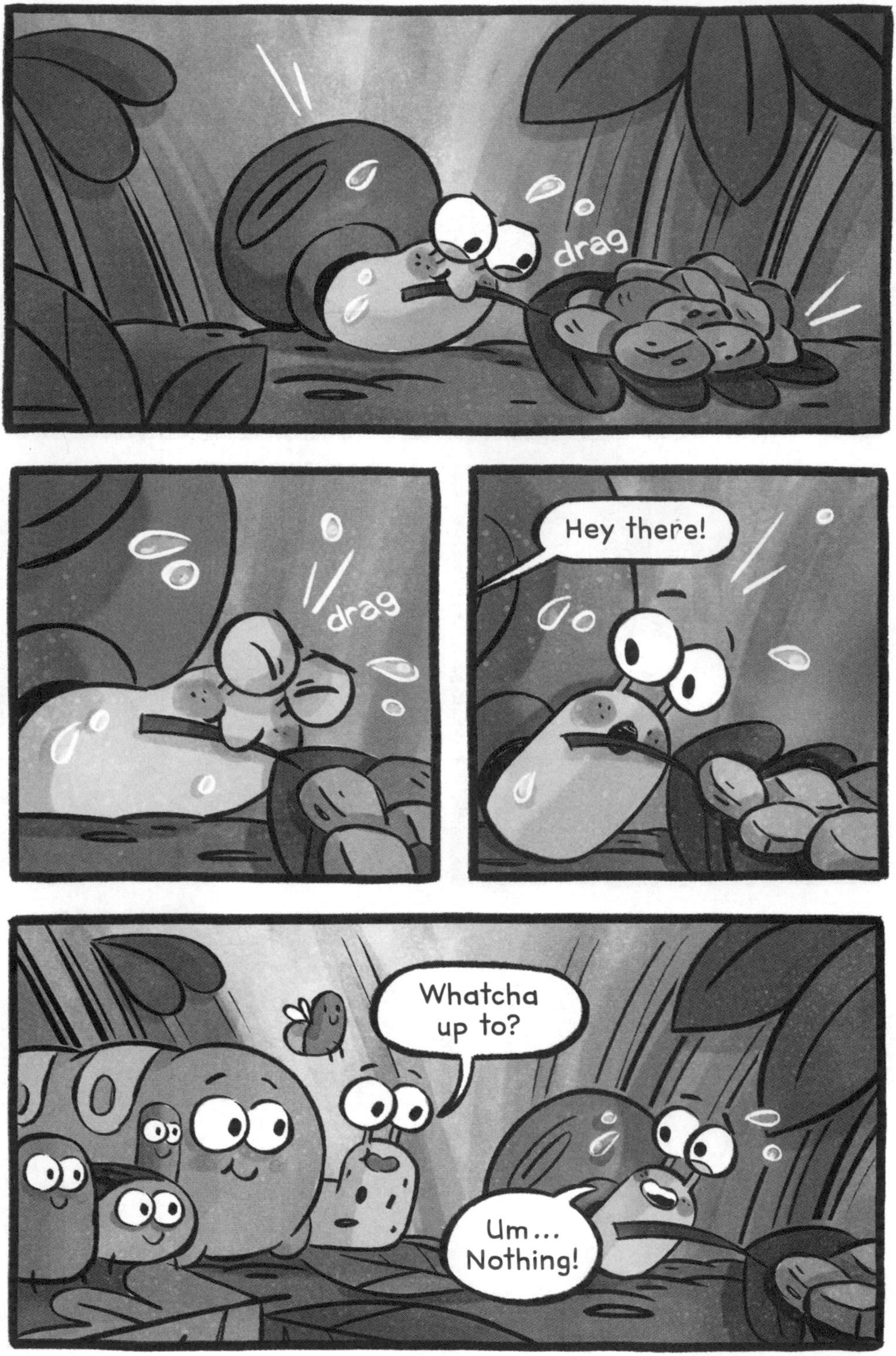
drag
drag
Hey there!
Whatcha up to?
Um... Nothing!

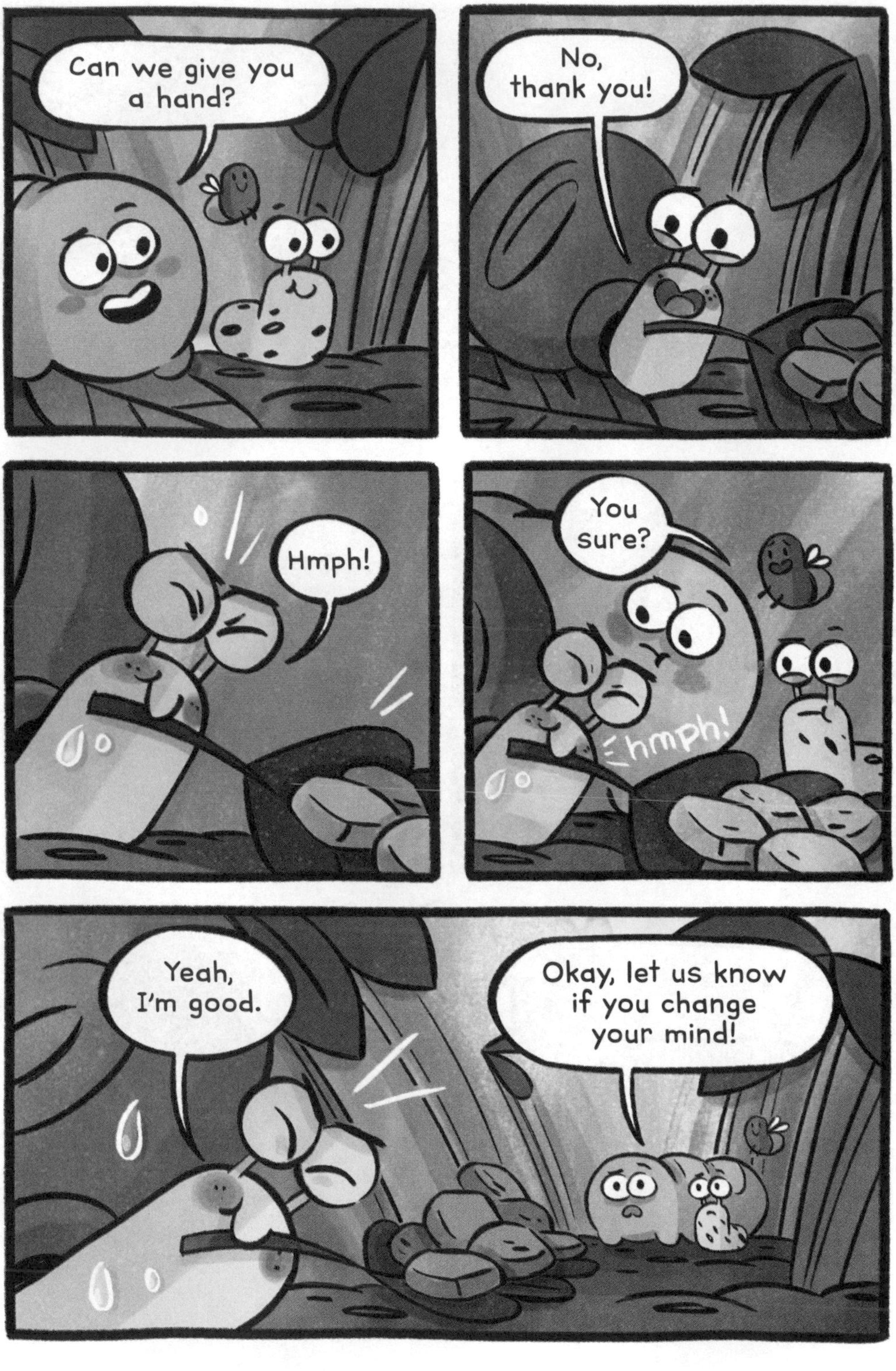
Can we give you a hand?
No, thank you!
Hmph!
You sure?
hmph!
Yeah, I'm good.
Okay, let us know if you change your mind!

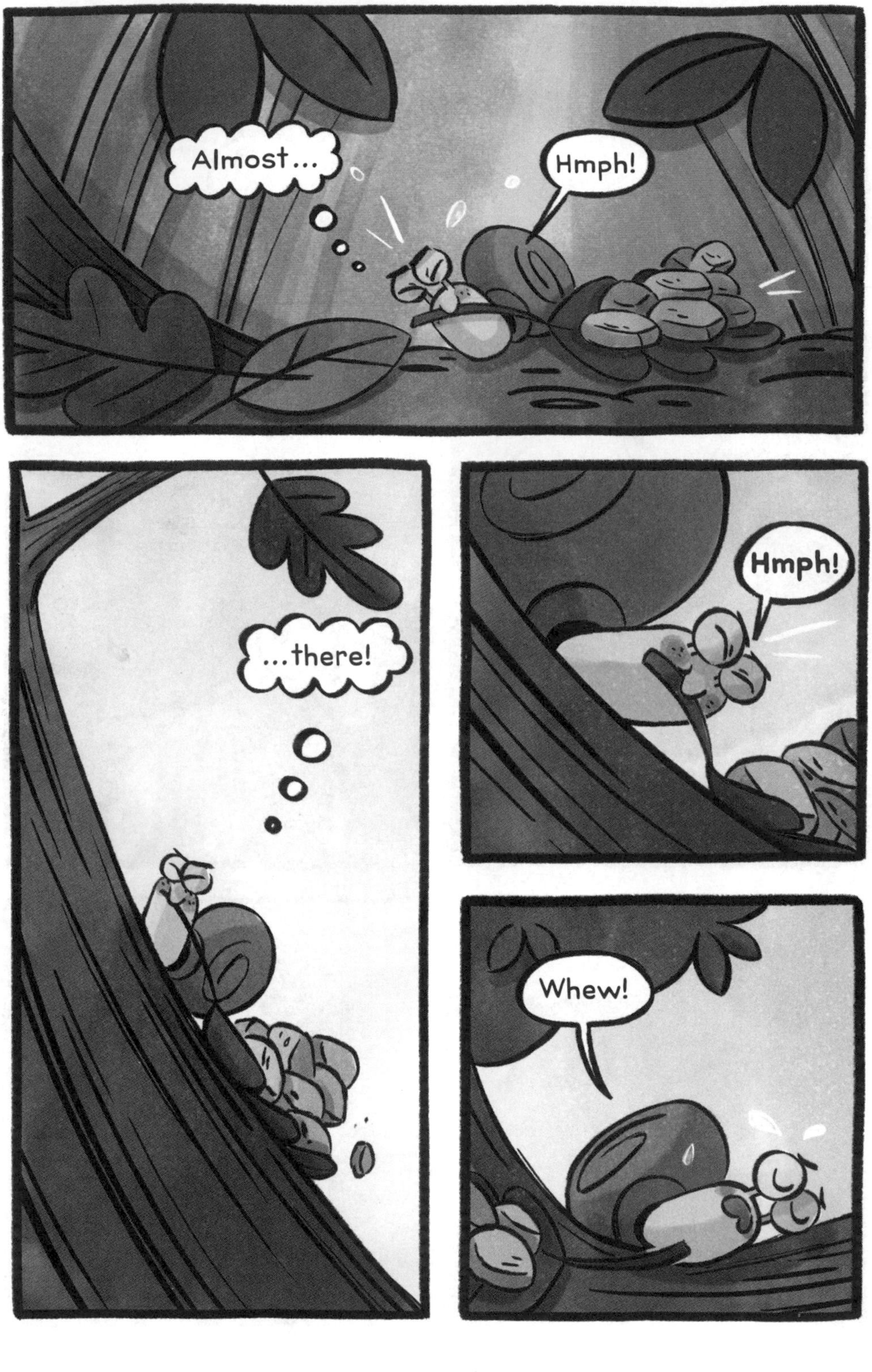
Almost...
Hmph!
...there!
Hmph!
Whew!

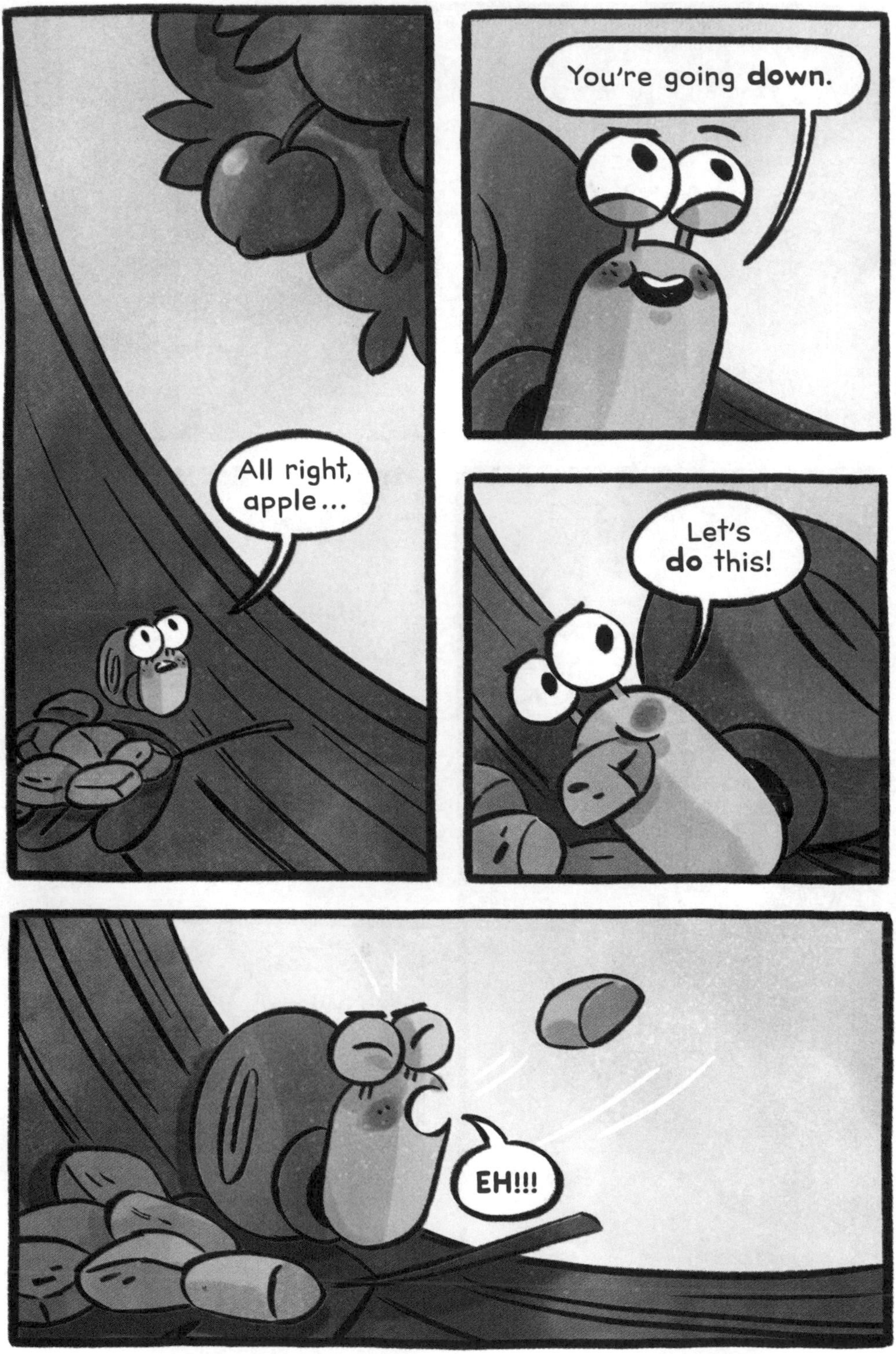
All right, apple...
You're going **down.**
Let's **do** this!
EH!!!

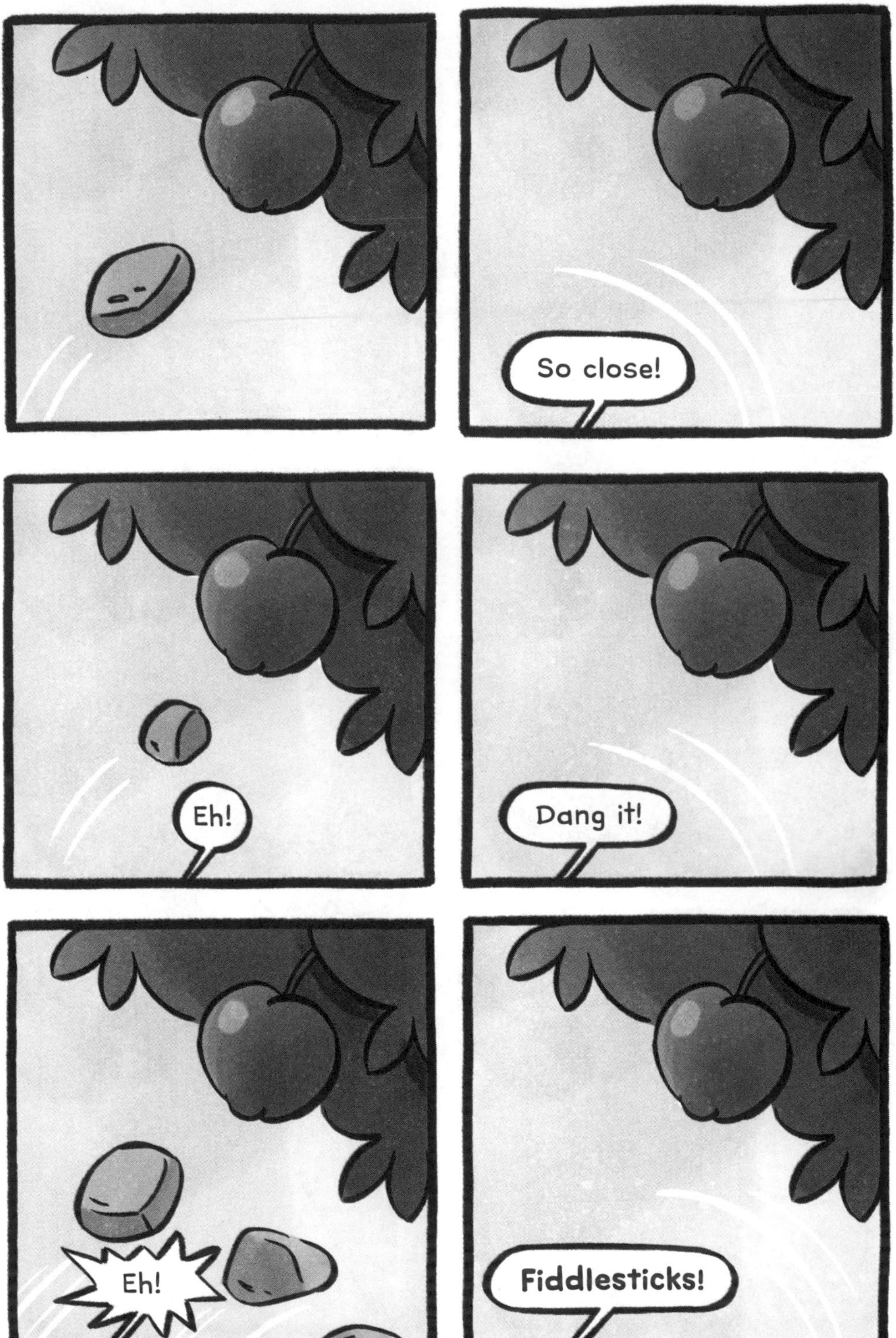
So close!
Eh!
Dang it!
Eh!
Fiddlesticks!

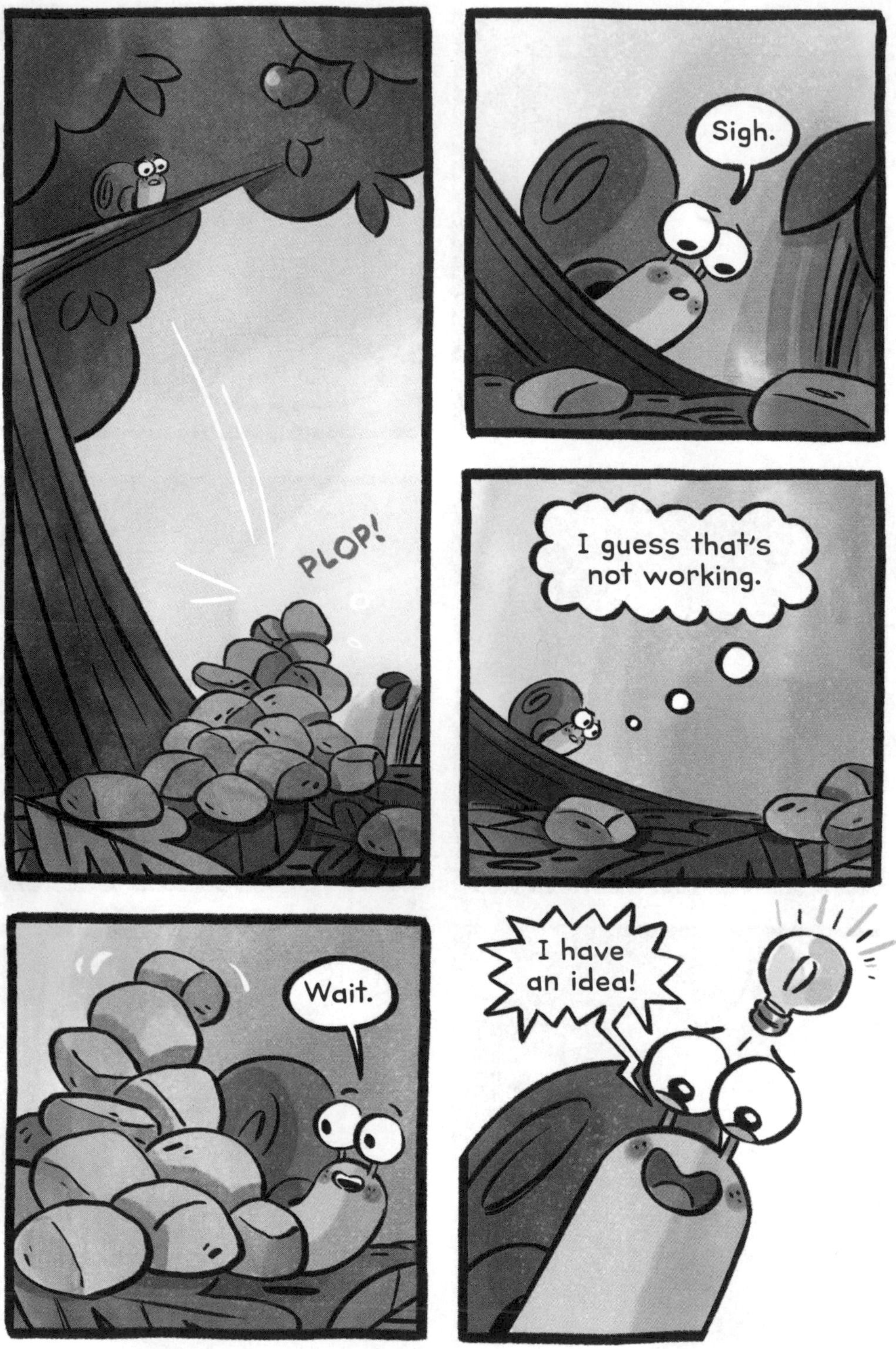
PLOP!
Sigh.
I guess that's not working.
Wait.
I have an idea!

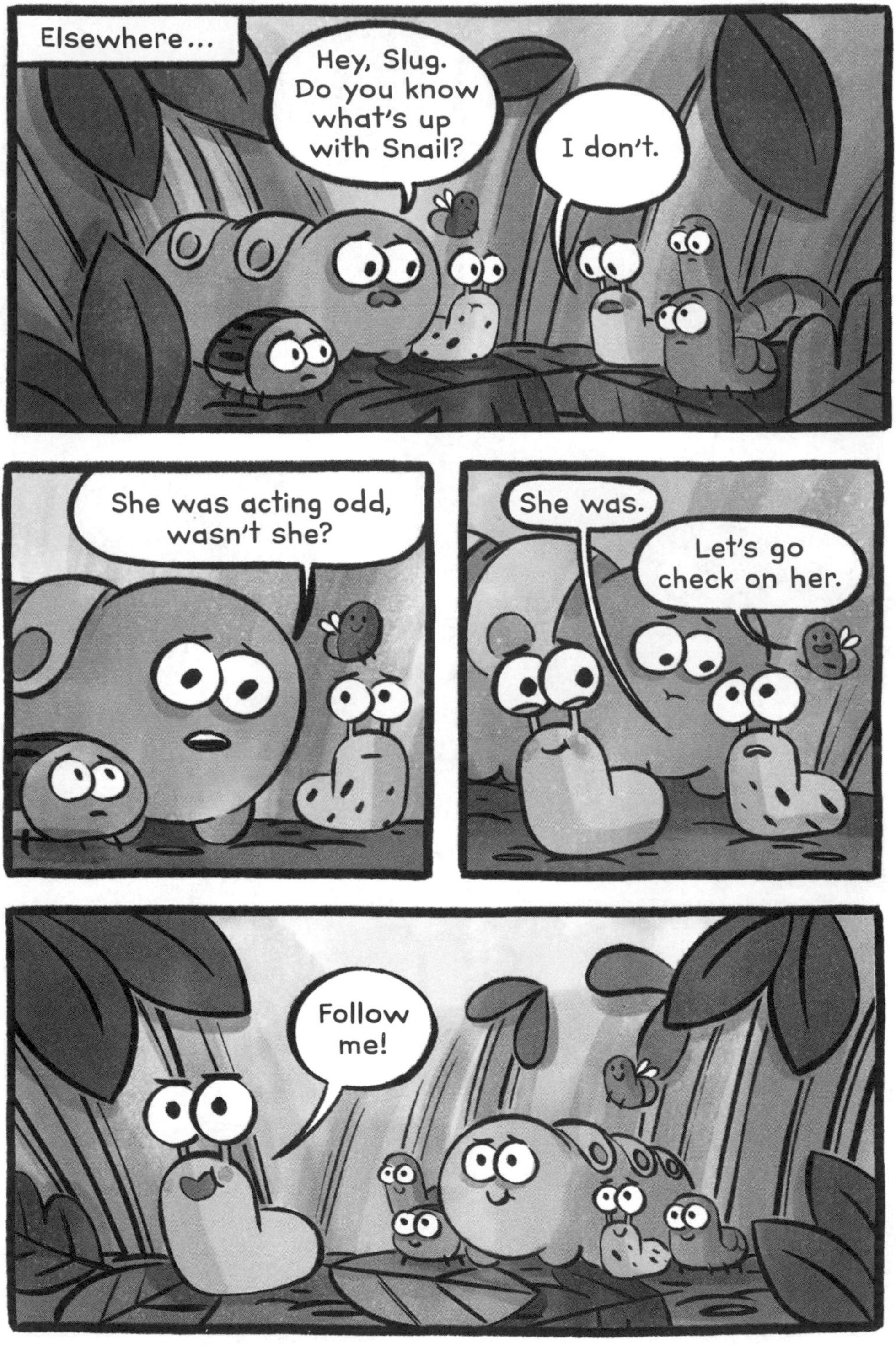
Elsewhere...
Hey, Slug. Do you know what's up with Snail?
I don't.
She was acting odd, wasn't she?
She was.
Let's go check on her.
Follow me!

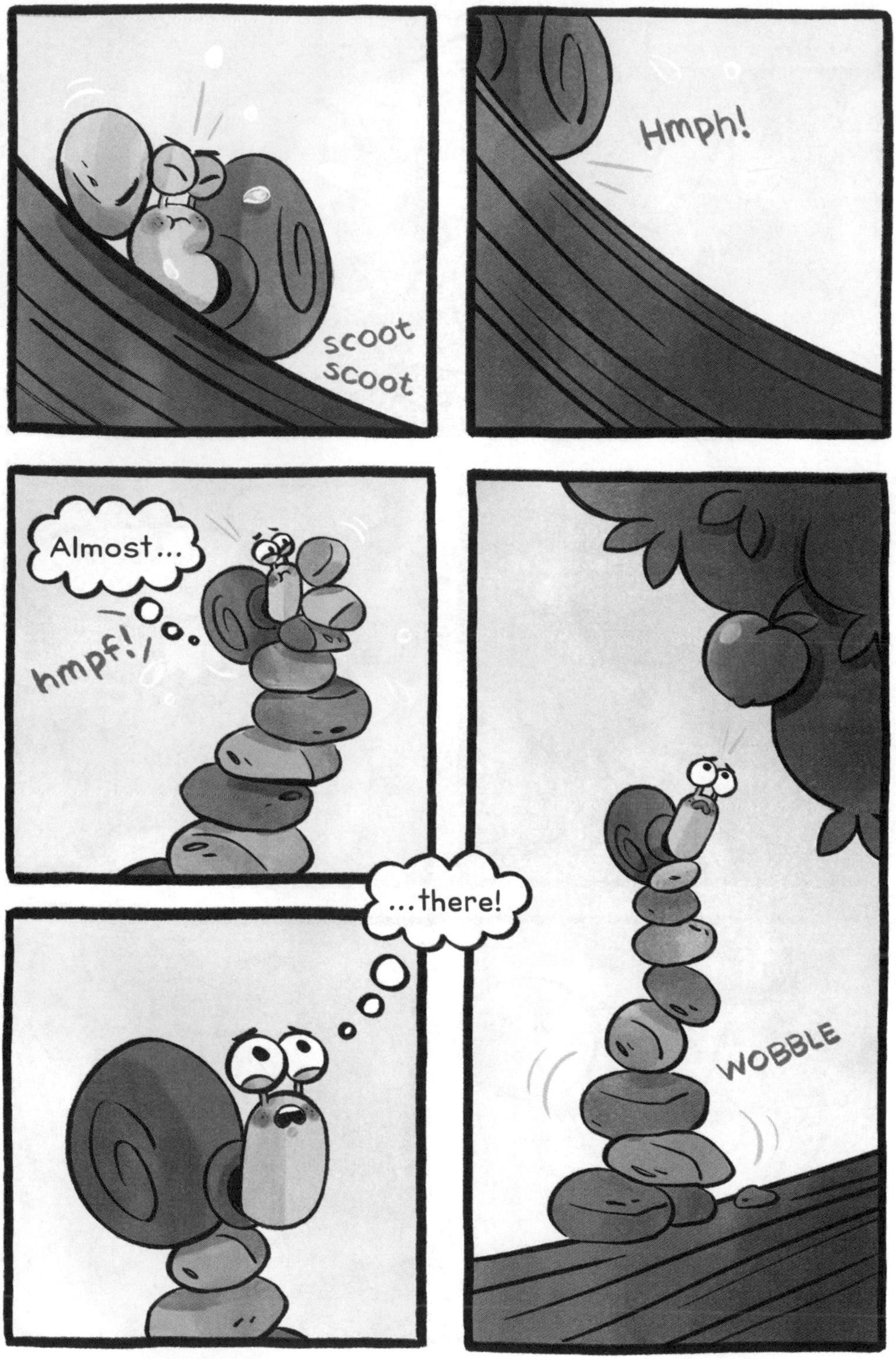
scoot
scoot
Hmph!
Almost...
hmpf!
...there!
WOBBLE

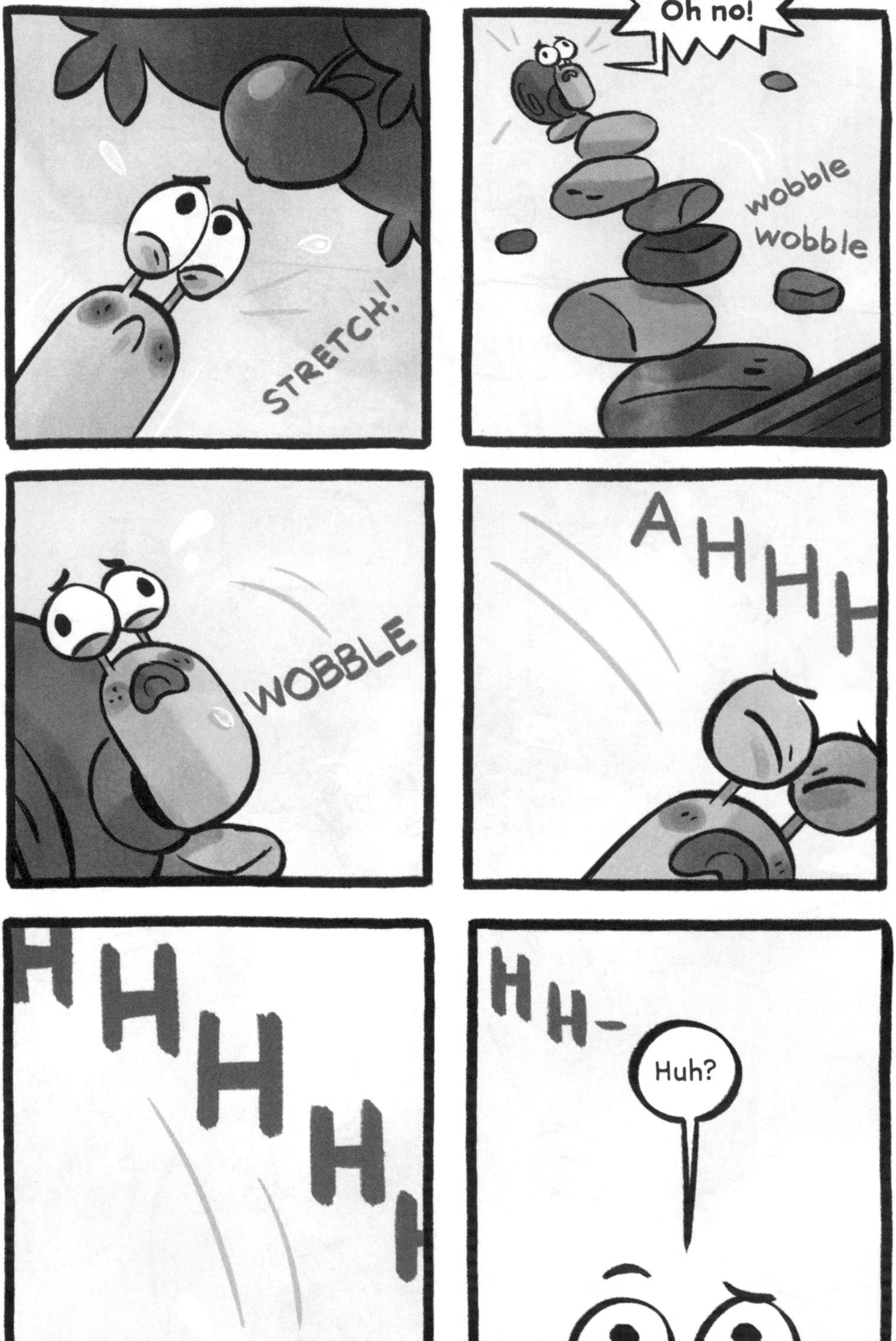
STRETCH!
Oh no!
wobble
wobble
WOBBLE
AHHH
HHHHH
HH-
Huh?

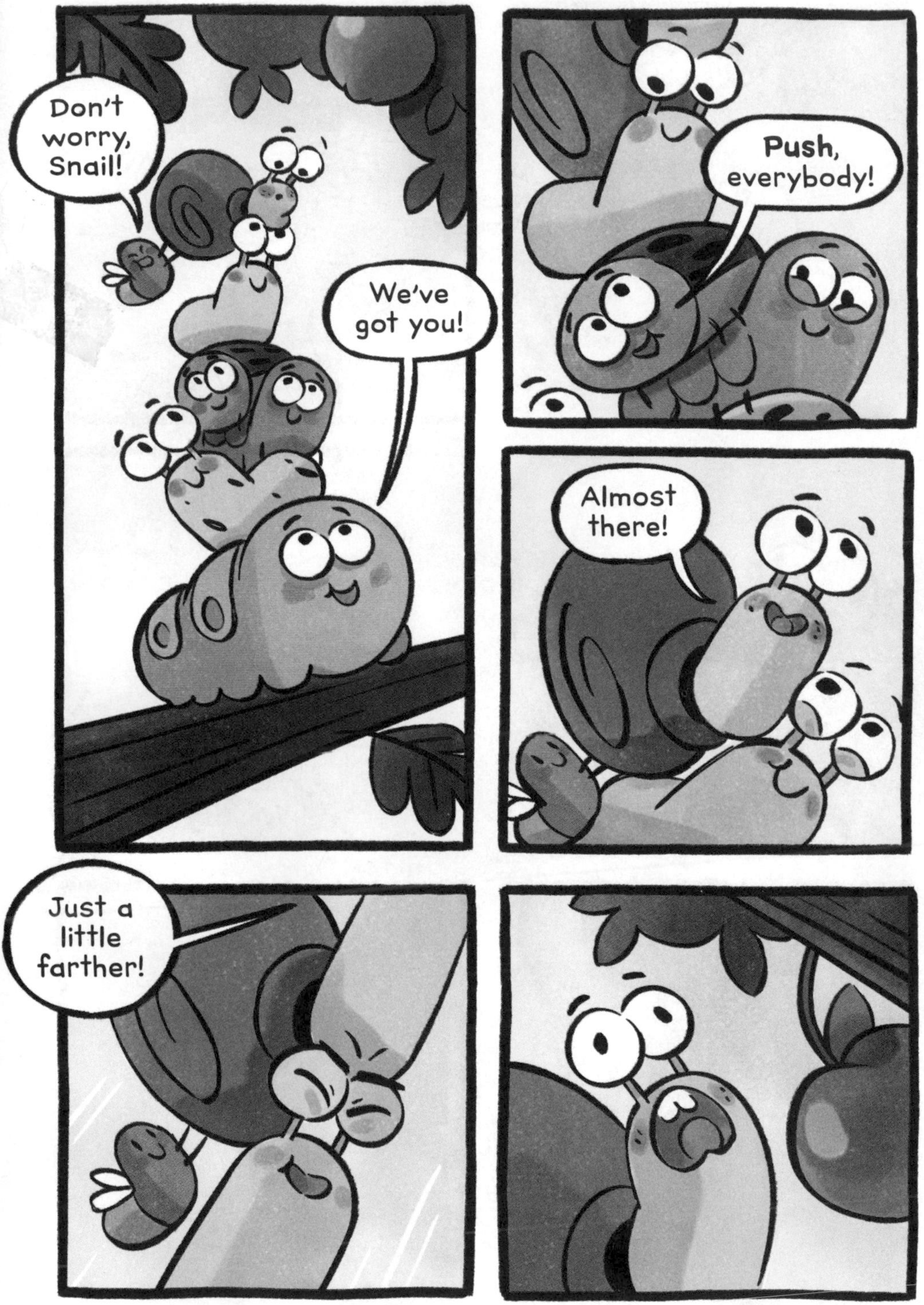
Don't worry, Snail!
We've got you!
Push, everybody!
Almost there!
Just a little farther!

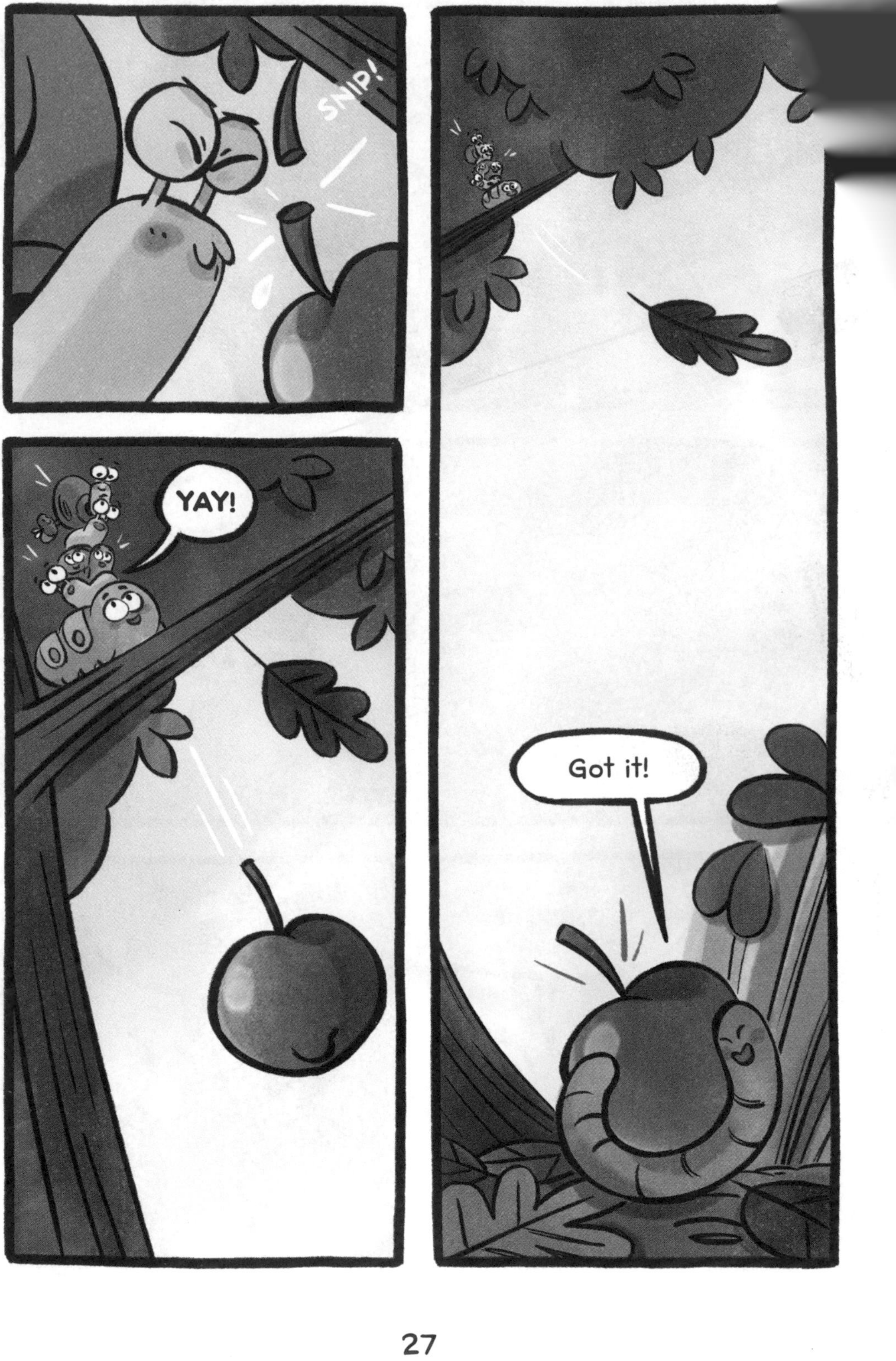
SNIP!
YAY!
Got it!

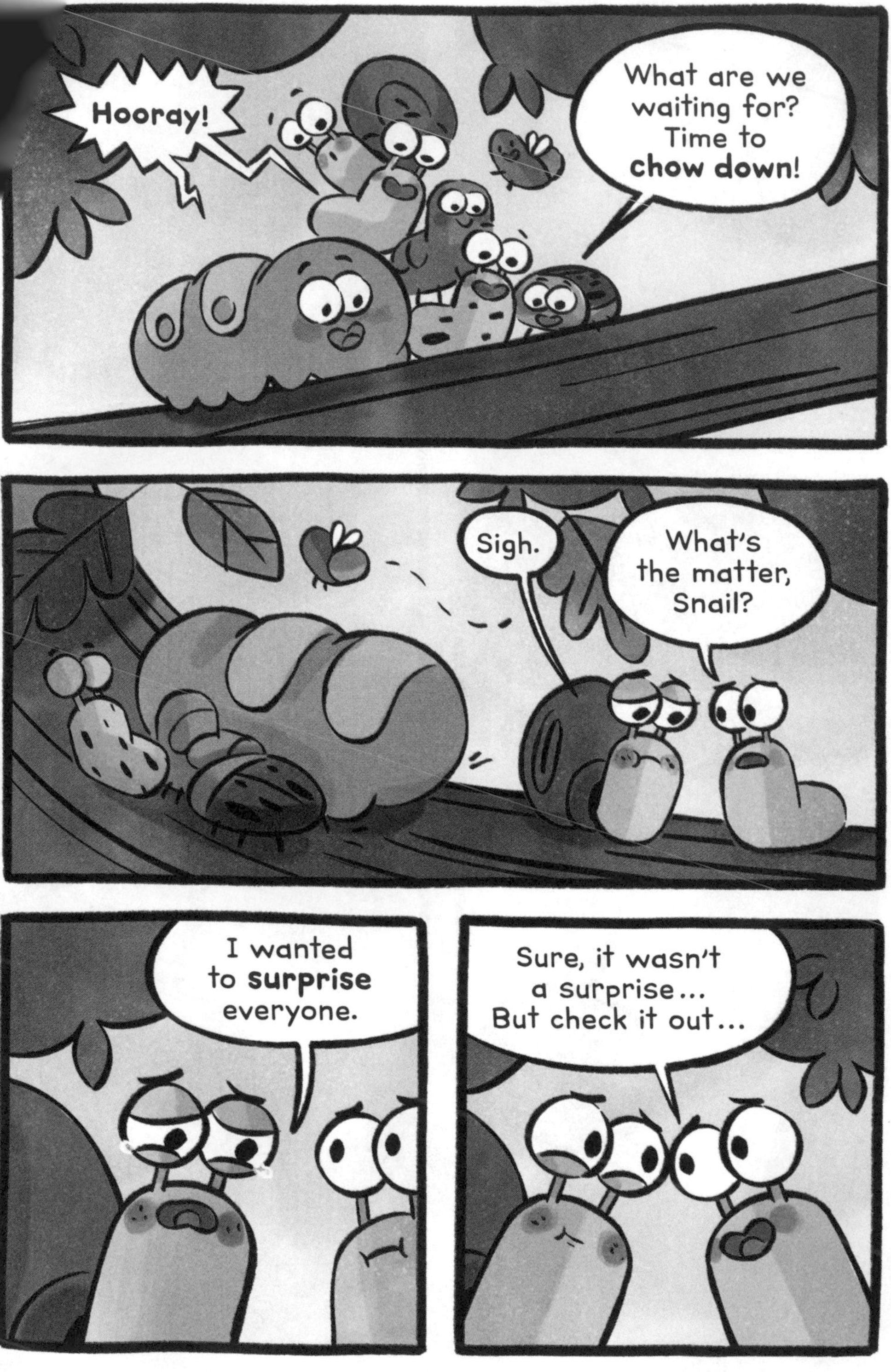
Hooray!
What are we waiting for? Time to **chow down**!
Sigh.
What's the matter, Snail?
I wanted to **surprise** everyone.
Sure, it wasn't a surprise... But check it out...

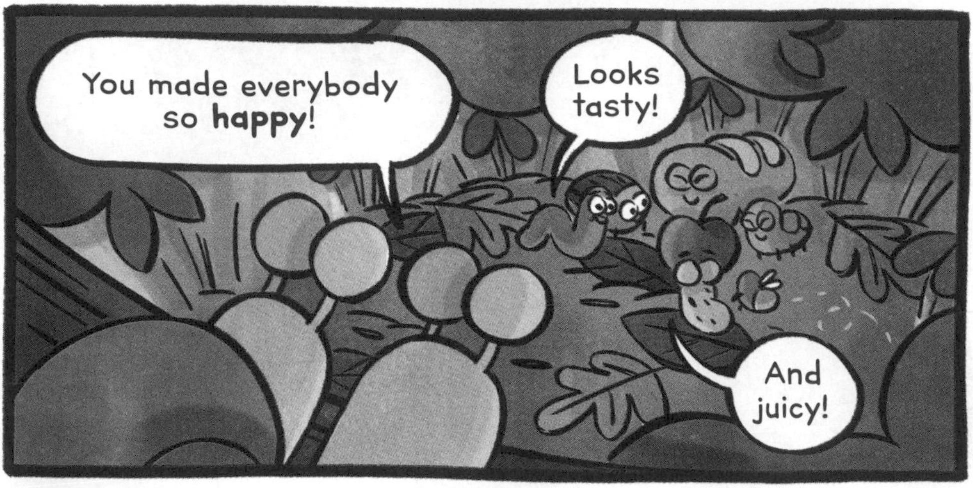
You made everybody so **happy**!
Looks tasty!
And juicy!

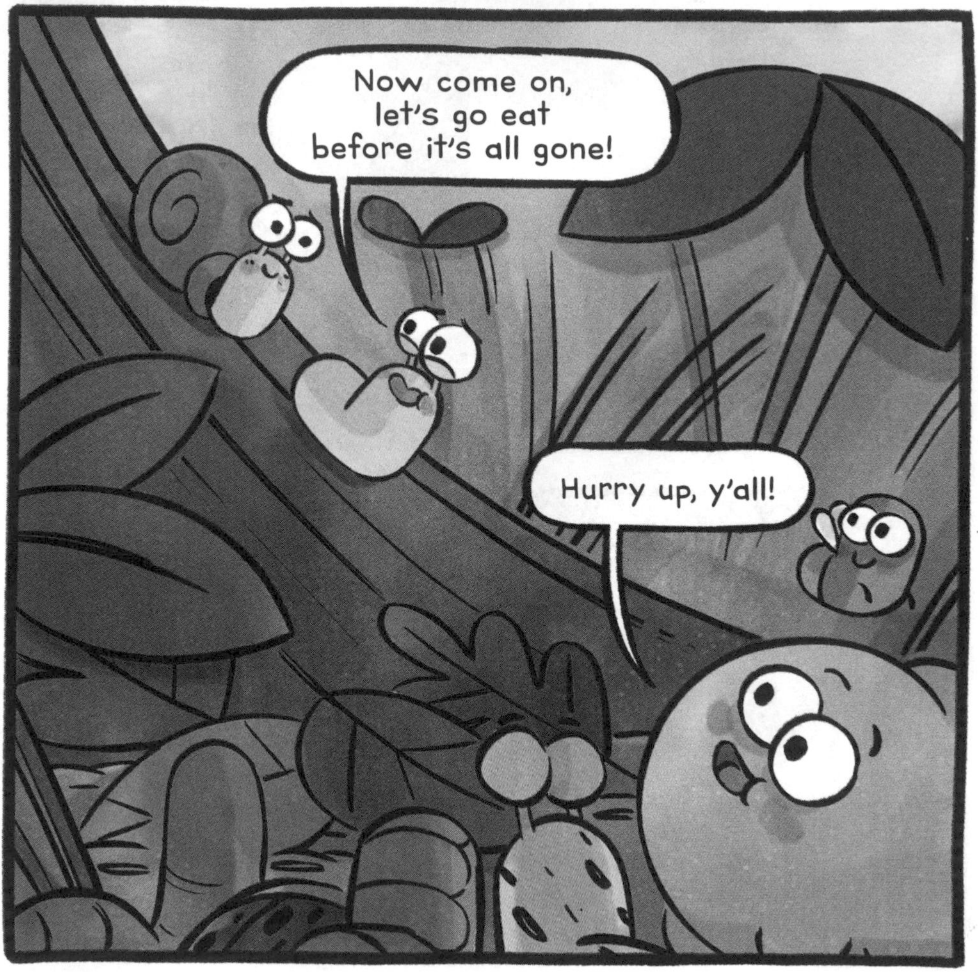
Now come on, let's go eat before it's all gone!
Hurry up, y'all!

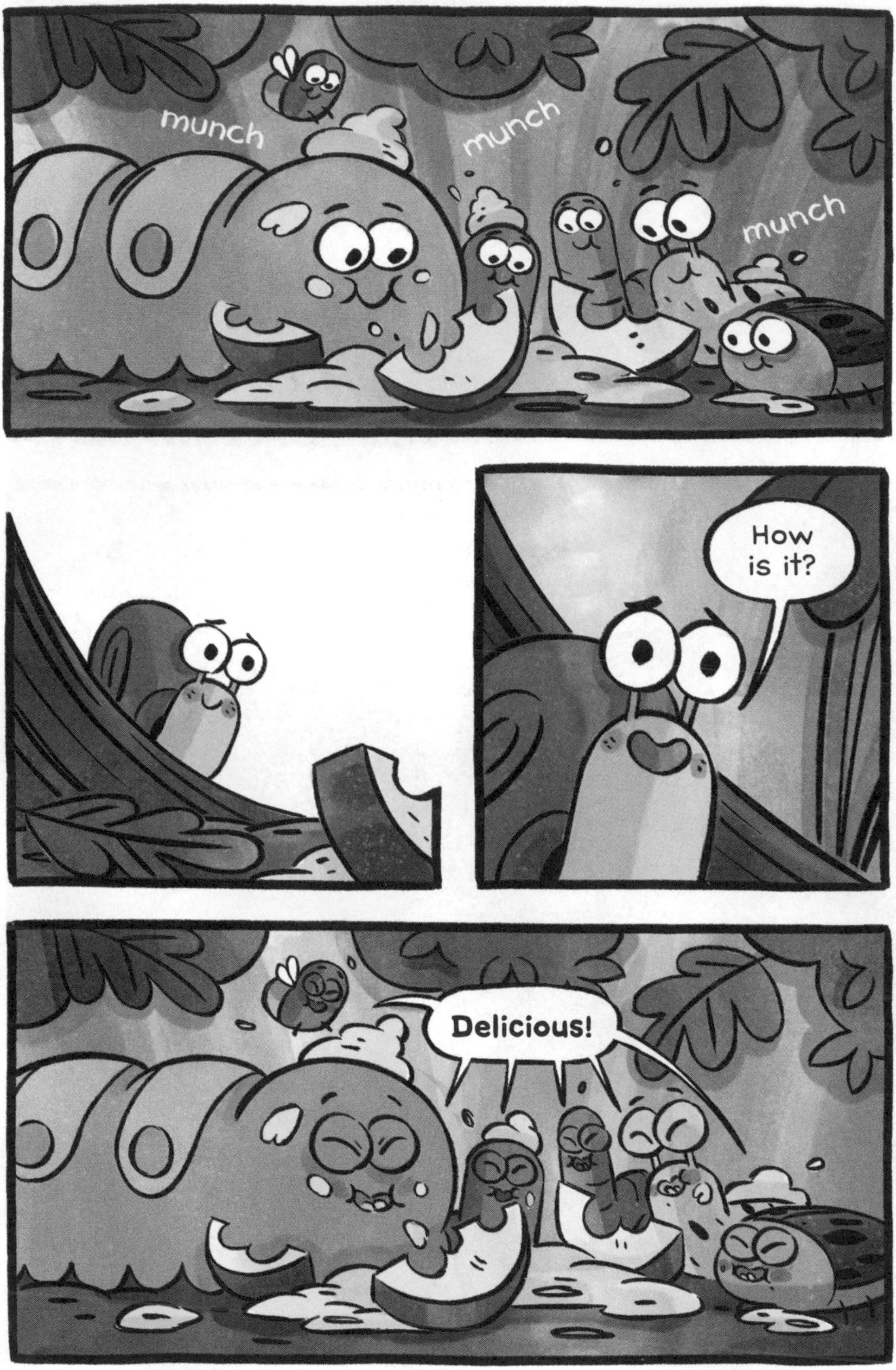
munch
munch
munch
How is it?
Delicious!

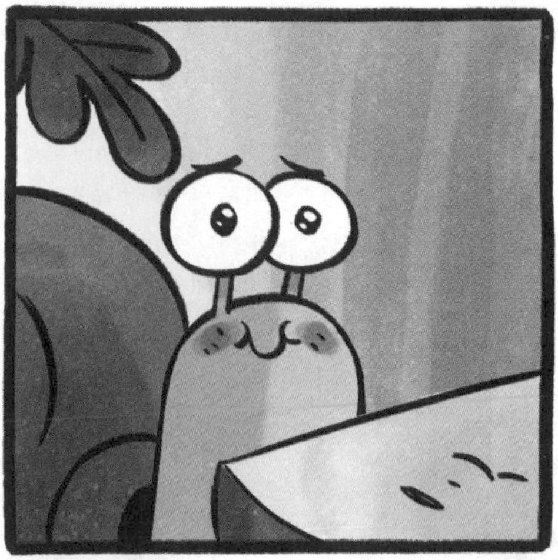

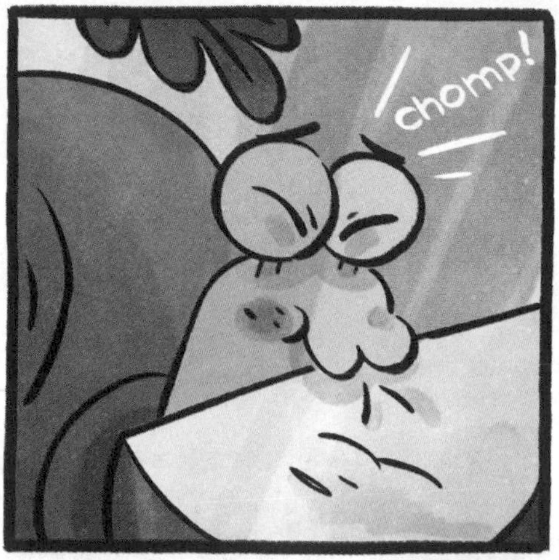
CHOMP!

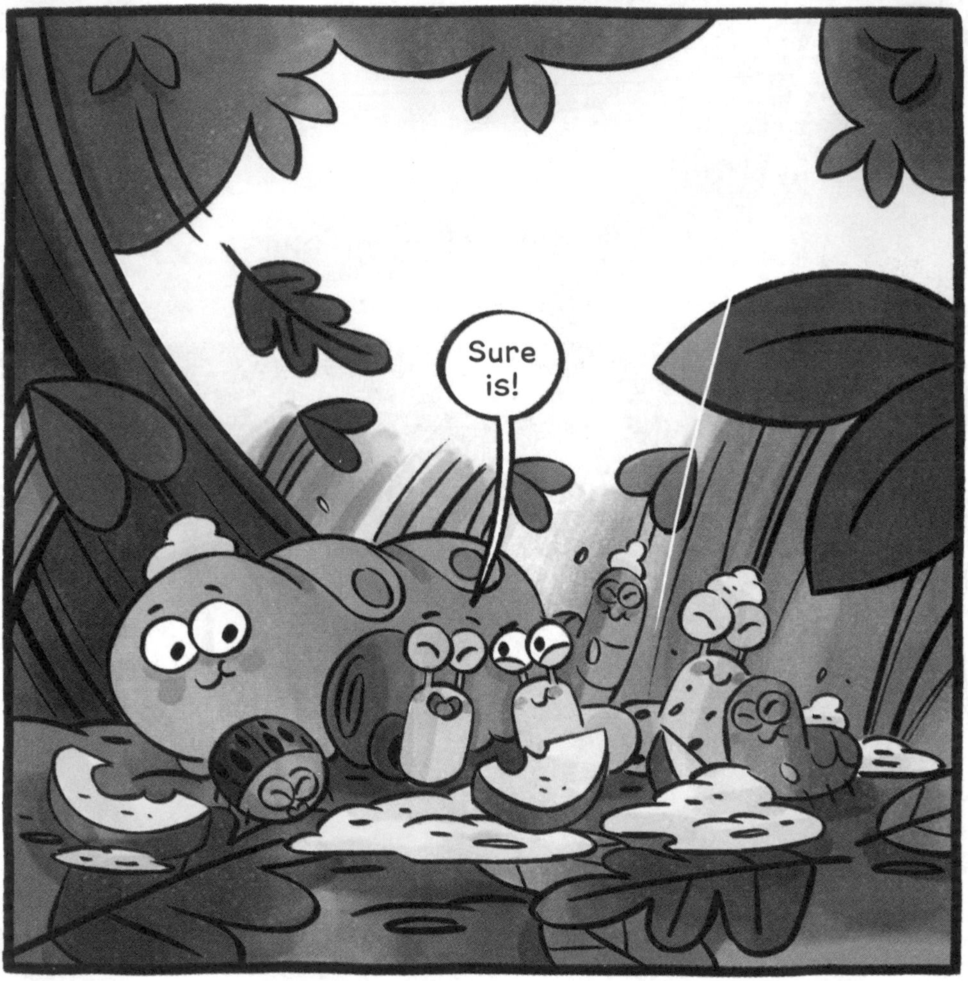
Sure is!

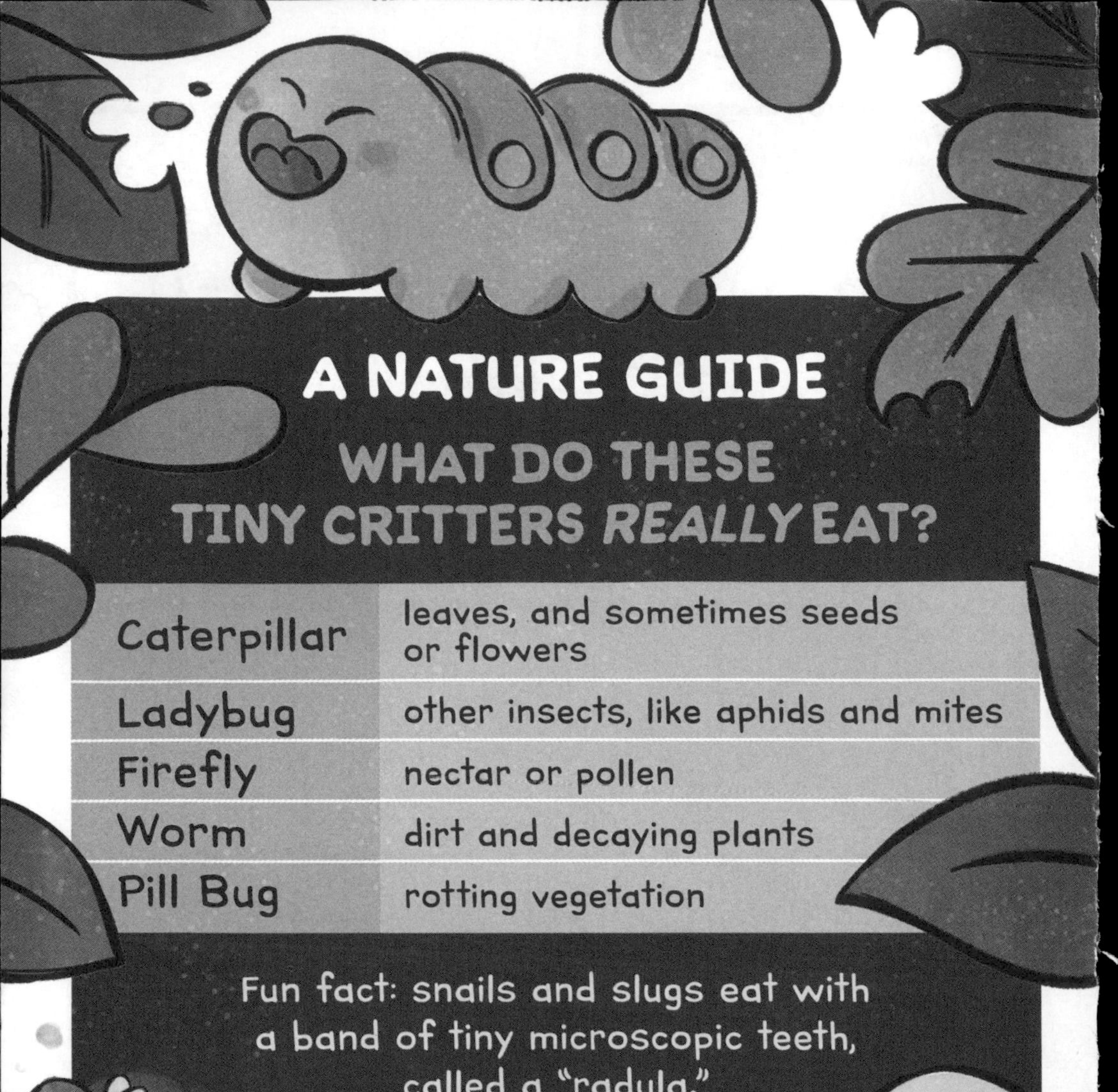

# A NATURE GUIDE

## WHAT DO THESE TINY CRITTERS *REALLY* EAT?

| | |
|---|---|
| Caterpillar | leaves, and sometimes seeds or flowers |
| Ladybug | other insects, like aphids and mites |
| Firefly | nectar or pollen |
| Worm | dirt and decaying plants |
| Pill Bug | rotting vegetation |

Fun fact: snails and slugs eat with a band of tiny microscopic teeth, called a "radula."

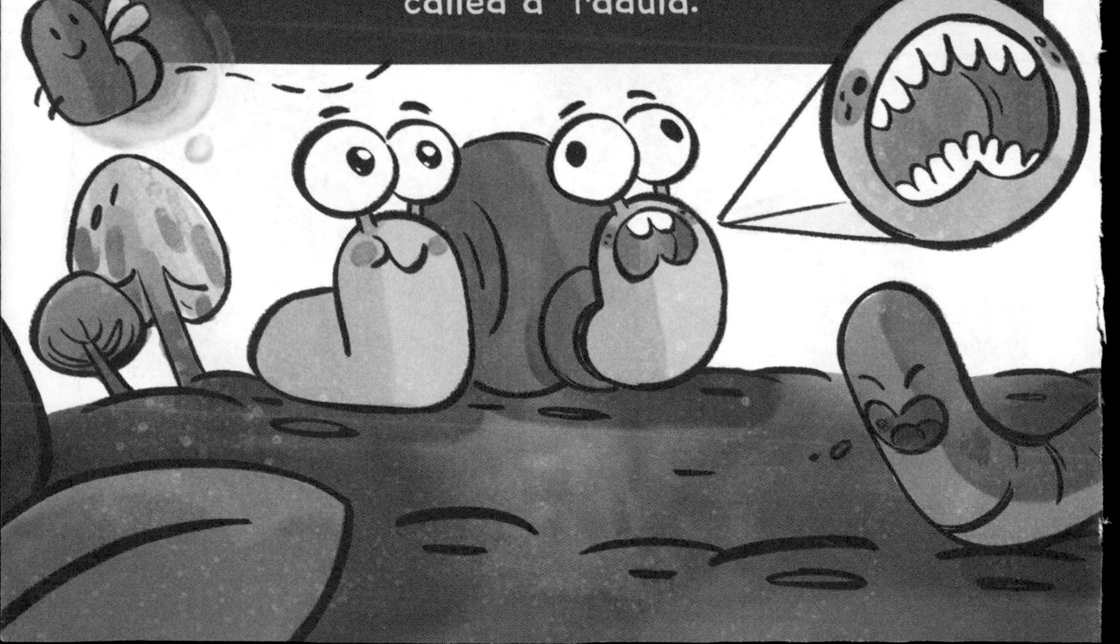